Simply
Irisistible
Isabella Proctor Cozy Mysteries
Book 6

Lisa Bouchard

LISA BOUCHARD

SIMPLY IRISISTIBLE

LISA BOUCHARD

For Paul, who supports all my dreams.

Chapter 1

I thought my life was difficult with one cat. Three were practically unbearable.

Don't get me wrong, it wasn't like I didn't love their cute, furry little hearts—but I swore to any goddess listening to me that if one of the kittens had another spellcasting "accident," and I wound up plastered to the ceiling again, I was going to have to ban them from my apartment. I didn't care how much Jameson complained.

I finished pulling out the yellow confetti that was stuck in my hair—courtesy of the kittens—and I was grateful it wasn't an exploded can of cat food, like last week.

Both were black kittens, but Jules had white feet, and Jessamin had a white-tipped tail. Jessamin ran into the living room, jumped on the couch, and leaped off toward the apartment door. She stayed where she landed and watched Jules make the same run. Jules beat Jessamin's distance by two paws, so Jules pounced on her sister.

They played this game repeatedly while they were here, and I wondered if they weren't trying to teach themselves how to fly.

"Hey, do you want me to make all this pasta?" Delia called from the kitchen.

I sat at the dining room table. "Sure. I don't mind eating leftovers later this week."

We were cooking in my apartment, because the aunts had gone to the Maine Magic and Crystals trade show for the weekend. They were looking to replenish supplies for Proctor House, and I had given them a list of hard-to-find ingredients and the maximum price I was willing to pay for each item. I wasn't ready to leave the apothecary to Mackenzie for two days straight, so I stayed home. I really should speed up my production of candles and bath products and start selling them at the trade show.

I didn't quite understand how the event worked but, somehow, non-witches weren't able to buy anything they could harm themselves with.

Grandma was in Sewall, spending a few days with Hope, so Thea, Delia, and I were on our own. Tonight we were having spaghetti with meatballs, but I had a backup plan of frozen pizza in case things didn't go well. Palmer had been working nights lately, so I wasn't able to talk him into taking pity on us and cooking dinner.

Thea was on the couch, petting Jameson and, whenever they would slow down enough, Jules and Jessamin. All in all, it was a lovely domestic scene in my apartment, and I was grateful for every peaceful moment of it.

Hope had finally convinced the sorority to accept me as a member last week, but things were calm even with them, because there had been no word of the Fraternity of Free Witches doing anything wrong. The fact we hadn't heard from them at all was worrying, but there wasn't anything to do except prepare for their next attack.

"Delia and I have decided we're going to hire an assistant," Thea said as Jules jumped off her lap to chase Jameson's Roomba-like toy.

I turned to her. "Really? That's great. What are you going to have them do?"

"Reception," Delia called from the kitchen. "If we didn't have to answer the phone and greet people coming in off the street, we could get a lot more done."

I bet they could. They ran Port City Tours and, in addition to working with customers, they developed their own tours, researched everything they talked about, and sewed their own tour-themed costumes. On busy weeks it was exhausting to watch them work. Unlike my apothecary, where I used magic in my potions, my cousins did not use any magic in their business. They didn't need to, and they felt a strict line of no magic was better for them.

"Where did you find Mackenzie?" Thea asked. "If we could find someone like her, that would be great."

I definitely lucked out when I hired Mackenzie. On paper, she looked like the least promising candidate, but once she got into the shop and we started talking, I knew she'd work out. "I posted a job ad on one of those online sites."

"How did you know she'd work out so well?" Delia asked.

I shrugged. "I didn't. Not until I met her. Now, I'm not sure what I'd do without her."

Jameson hopped off the couch and called to his nieces. They stopped playing and followed him into his room.

"Weird," Thea said, watching them walk in a line down the hallway.

Jameson's bedroom door closed. "Worrying," I said. "It's like when you babysit and you can't hear the kid anymore, you know something bad is happening."

"Can I get some help in here?" Delia asked.

"Yeah, sure. What do you need?" Thea asked as she walked into the kitchen.

"Take the garlic bread out of the oven and, Isabella, you can set the table."

Five minutes later, we were eating the best meal we'd ever made on our own. "Maybe we're getting the hang of cooking," I said.

Delia laughed. "I don't think so. But we've learned which canned and premade foods we like best. I'm not sure I'll ever be as good a cook as my mother."

A loud crack sounded from Jameson's room. "Hey! Don't bother the neighbors," I called to him. When he didn't answer, I walked down the hall and opened his door. Bright green smoke billowed out of the room while Jameson, Jessamin, and Jules walked out as though nothing was wrong.

"Get rid of that smoke, would you?" Jameson asked me. You'd think that because he was my familiar, he'd do what I told him, but often it was the other way around.

Delia used her magic to open a window and blow the smoke outside. When it was all gone, she pointed her index finger at the open window and moved it down. The window closed, keeping the rest of the chilly December air out. "What was that?"

Jessamin started to meow. The kittens had moved to Proctor House six weeks ago, on Samhain, and could communicate with Thea and Delia. I was still out of the loop though.

Thea laughed. "She thought we might not notice."

I turned to the kitten. Even though I couldn't understand her, she had never had a problem knowing what any of us said. "You thought we wouldn't notice a thunderclap and green smoke? Seriously?"

Jameson licked his paw. "I told her you were smarter than most humans, but she insisted we wait to see."

Jules began to meow, and Delia translated for me. "Jules says she doubts it, and that you still have confetti in your hair."

Shoot! I thought I'd pulled it all out. "That's it. The kittens need to go home after dinner. For now, I want the two of you sitting quietly where I can see you." I turned to Jameson. "What exactly are you teaching them? How to pounce on my last nerve?"

He looked up at me and yawned. How rude! "I am teaching them how to get along with humans. They're mastering everything I give them faster than any other trainees I've ever had. They'll be ready to take on their duties as familiars in another six months, and they need to test the boundaries of what humans will accept."

Jules and Jessamin sat quietly by the front door, doing their best to look innocent. I wasn't buying it. "Way past the line, girls. Way past."

We sat back down to finish dinner and out of the corner of my eye, I saw Jules batting at Jessamin. "Jules," I said, sounding just like my mother when she warned me to behave when I was small.

"Six months, you say?" Delia asked Jameson.

Thea and Delia had become attached to the kittens, and I knew they would be heartbroken if Jessamin and Jules chose to be familiars for other witches when the time came. Delia, in particular, had ramped up her spellcasting practice in the hope she'd be strong enough to merit a familiar. As annoying as the kittens were today, even I hoped they'd stay with the family. I wished I had advice for my cousins on how to get a familiar, but my former neighbor Mrs. Thompson had chosen me for Jameson, and I had never figured out why.

I jumped at a loud bang on my apartment door. I looked to the kittens, but they weren't responsible for this noise.

Someone knocked on the door again with more force than was necessary. I looked through the peephole and saw my new neighbor scowling at the door. I turned to the kittens. "Great, now you've upset the neighbors. Don't you move while I'm talking to him."

I opened the door. "Hi, Bruce. What can I do for you?"

Bruce worked from home and always seemed to be working, because he insisted on the building being quiet all the time. Apparently he didn't do many video calls, because I doubted his stained T-shirt with expletives all over it was workplace appropriate anywhere. "You can quit making so much noise. The landlord assured me this was a quiet building and that you, in particular, were a quiet person that I'd never have any problems with."

I certainly tried to be a good neighbor, but the kittens were making it difficult. I smiled at the thought of Mr. S. neglecting to mention the building fire and my part in it as he talked up my qualities as a neighbor. I am fairly quiet, but maybe Mr. S. was stretching the truth a little bit to convince Bruce to take the apartment. I looked at my watch. "You can't possibly still be working, it's seven o'clock."

"It doesn't matter if I'm working or not, you're being too loud. I'd hate to complain to the landlord about you, but if this keeps up, I will. It would be a shame if you and that bad luck cat of yours had to move, just before Christmas."

Jameson hissed, not happy to be called "bad luck."

"Are you even allowed to have a pet? I'll ask him that too."

I wasn't happy about where his veiled threats were leading, but I was confident Mr. S. wouldn't throw me out—not after I'd found out one of his tenants was a kidnapper, and also apprehended the murderer of another tenant. Still, Bruce didn't know that, and there was no reason to tell him.

"We'll try to be more quiet," I said.

Bruce took a step forward, as though he were going to push his way into the living room. I stood back as if to invite him in, confident in the wards my family had placed around my apartment. His foot passed over the threshold and the expression on his face changed from angry to confused. He withdrew his foot and looked at me. "Sorry, what?" he asked.

Say what you like about witches, but we could put up some fantastic wards. The wards on my apartment left a person confused as to why they were there and with a vague feeling like they ought to go home.

I smiled. "You asked me to be quieter, and I agreed to try."

"Oh, right. Ah, thanks," he said before he turned and walked down the hall to his door.

I closed my door and leaned against it. He'd never tried to come in before, and the expression on his face before he hit the protective ward wasn't one I ever wanted to see again.

"You need to talk to your landlord about him," Thea said.

I sighed. "I know. I'll go down when you leave."

We cleaned up after dinner, and I walked my cousins and their kittens out to the car. As they drove off, I wondered how I could diplomatically complain about a neighbor who would probably be complaining about me soon.

I knocked on the Subramanians' door and Mrs. S. opened it. "Oh, Isabella, come in please."

Every time I went into their apartment, I was intimidated. They had white furniture that I was certain I'd leave a stain on. Even though I didn't make the sauce, I could have some on me and then I'd ruin their couch. "Is your husband here?"

She shook her head. "No. He had a call and rushed out. He said it was an emergency with one of the men on his bowling team."

"Oh, I'm sorry to hear that."

"I can tell him you stopped by," she offered.

"That would be great, thanks."

As I walked back to my apartment, careful to tiptoe past Bruce's apartment door, I thought about the emergency. Mr. S. was on a bowling team, but I also knew he lied about some bowling practice times and visited his son, daughter-in-law, and grandson instead. For a brief moment, he had been a suspect in a murder investigation and I followed him, only to find out he was visiting family but not telling his wife. Since then, Mrs. S. had met her grandson and family reconciliation had started

LISA BOUCHARD

Chapter 2

I unlocked the apothecary the next morning, still not having spoken to Mr. S. His car wasn't in the lot when I left, so I resolved to call him during a slow stretch in the afternoon.

I had a morning routine that I didn't deviate from. I hung up my coat and bag, changed out of my boots, and put a new candle in the holder next to Trina's photo. Trina had been my mentor and the former owner of the apothecary. It wasn't until after she'd been murdered that I learned she left me her business. There wasn't a day that went by that I wasn't grateful for her generosity and her friendship.

I snapped my fingers and her candle lit. I'd taken to talking to her in the mornings, bringing her up to speed on what was happening in the shop. I knew it was silly; if her ghost was here, she already knew, and if it wasn't, she couldn't hear me. I wasn't ready to give up my emotional connection to her yet. "Mackenzie is working out well. You should see how tidy the shop is now—she puts both of us to shame."

Next on my list was to brew the tea I'd be serving customers throughout the day. I looked at the shelves and decided on double dark chocolate maté. A storm was going to blow in this afternoon, and I was sure my customers would appreciate the robust chocolate flavor.

I flew through the rest of my morning tasks on autopilot, thinking about my neighbor Bruce and wondering if Mr. Subramanian had worked out his bowling emergency.

At ten o'clock, I opened the shop to customers. Mrs. Scanlon got out of her car and hurried into the warm shop. She took a deep breath. "Chocolate?"

I grinned. "Double dark chocolate. It seemed like that kind of day. Can I pour you some?"

She took the mug I handed her. "What have you got for someone who can't seem to stay warm?"

I looked at her for a moment and allowed my intuition to tell me what she needed. Cinnamon, ginger, and turmeric with a base of chamomile leaves. "Let me whip something up for you." I pulled the jars I needed off the shelves and weighed out a week's worth of tea for her.

"How warm do you keep your house?" I asked, knowing many older people lower their heat to save money.

"Sixty-seven. But I'm cold even if I turn it up."

I handed her the bag of tea. "Have a mug of this after breakfast and another after dinner. This should last you a week and, if it works, you can come back for more."

She smiled. "Thank you, dear. I think I'll take some of this chocolate tea too."

I put her teas in a bag and sent her off, hoping she'd be warmer now. My intuition had yet to fail me, so I thought she'd be fine and I'd see her in a week.

Half an hour later, my landlord came in. I smiled at him as he brushed snow off his jacket. "You didn't have to come in, we could have talked on the phone."

He looked up from his jacket. "What?"

"I should have told your wife it wasn't urgent and you could call me whenever it was convenient for you."

"You spoke to Nila? When was this?" he asked.

"I stopped by last night. She didn't tell you?"

He shook his head. "No. I haven't been home since last night."

I took a moment to look carefully at him. "You look like something's wrong. Let me pour you a mug of tea, and we can talk in my office."

I poured two mugs and we went into my office. "Why don't you tell me why you're here," I suggested.

He set his mug on my desk and when he looked up at me, his eyes were brimming with tears. "It's my son, Prashad. He's been arrested for murder, and I know he'd never kill anyone."

I wondered briefly if the parents of murderers also had that thought, or did they reflect and consider that yes, maybe their kid could have murdered someone. I shook my head. The Subramanians were gentle people, and I doubted they'd raised a murderer.

"That's horrible! I'm so sorry to hear this. But I'm not sure I can help you."

He took a deep breath. "You can. He was arrested by your friend, Detective Palmer."

No wonder he hadn't called me last night. I assumed he'd been busy, but I'm sure he also wanted to avoid telling me he'd arrested my landlord's son.

17

"I know there are rules, but my son won't do well in jail. Can you ask him to keep an eye on Prashad, to keep him safe. As soon as bail is set, we'll pay it, but until then . . . I worry."

"Of course I can call him and ask what he can do. He's also allowed to have visitors, so you and your wife can spend a good part of the day with him."

His face went pale. "No, you mustn't tell my wife. She can't know anything about this."

I raised an eyebrow.

"Nila and Prashad have had some problems since he got married," Mr. S. confided. "She had other matches in mind."

Prashad's wife was a lovely woman named Heather. She was a librarian, and you'd never met a kinder person.

"Let me get this straight. You don't want me to tell her that Prashad has been arrested? Don't you think she'll notice when he's not at the next family dinner?" I asked.

Mr. S. looked at me, fear and desperation warring on his face. "I'm counting on you to find out who did this, so my son can be set free before that happens."

"Okay, I can keep that secret. I'll call the detective and I'll let you know what he says."

Mr. S. stood up and shook my hand. "Thank you. Please remind him that I let him into your apartment so he could assemble your furniture."

I gave him my most reassuring smile. "He's not the kind of man to forget when someone does him a favor. I'm sure you have a lot to do today, so I won't keep you. If there's anything else I can do, please call me."

In the shop, I picked up a tin of chamomile and lavender tea. "Please, take this. Have some when you get home, you'll feel much better."

He reached for his wallet, but I couldn't let him pay for the tea, not after he'd been so good to me. "On the house."

At the door, he turned back to me. "I didn't ask you why you came to see me."

I'd completely forgotten about Bruce as soon as he'd told me his problem. "It's nothing, honestly. Bruce complained that I was too loud last night. He said he was going to talk to you about it, so I wanted to tell you I'd be more careful in the future."

"Don't you worry about him. I'll set him straight, and he won't complain about you again."

He left, and I wondered if my access to Palmer had just acted like a bribe to keep Bruce from bothering me. I didn't like that idea, but there was nothing I could do about it now.

Mackenzie arrived minutes later with coffee and bear claws from the Fancy Tart. Some days, having coffee and pastry delivered at noon was the best part of my day, and absolutely worth every penny I paid Mackenzie. She looked into my eyes. "You don't look so great."

I tried to brush off my concern for Prashad. "I'm fine. I'm just worried about my landlord's son. I've got to call Palmer and see if I can get something sorted out for him."

"I saw him at the Tart. We coordinated orders so we didn't bring you the same thing. He'll be here in a few minutes."

Excellent. It was always easier to talk about things in person. "What's in the bag?"

She handed me one of the bags she was holding, and a large hot cup. "Bear claw. And you've got a hot mocha as well."

"Sounds great. I don't have any special tasks for you today, so you watch the shop while I figure out what to say to Detective Palmer."

She winced. "Good luck with that."

In my office, I sat and closed my eyes. Being honest and forthright was the only way to go, but how to start? Before I could really get my mind around what I needed to say, there was a knock at my door.

"Are you busy?" Palmer asked, fruit tart in his hand.

I grinned at him. "Never too busy for a fancy tart."

He set the tart on my desk and sat down. "I've got some bad news about your landlord."

I leaned forward. "Mr. S. left just a few minutes ago, he told me. What makes you think his son is a murderer?"

Palmer sighed. "The evidence leads directly to him. He was overheard having a fight with the victim Thursday night, and the murder weapon was a heavy object from his desk. If he had any kind of alibi—anything at all—I'd have doubt, but since he doesn't, there's nothing I can do."

"Mr. S. wanted me to talk to you. He's worried for Prashad and thinks he'll have a difficult time in jail."

"We don't make it easy for a reason, you know."

I bit my lip. "Of course not, but you know the family a little bit, and you know how kind they've been to me. Is there anything you can do, at least until he makes bail?"

Palmer leaned back in his chair. "It's a murder charge, Isabella. There's no guarantee he'll even get bail, much less be able to afford it."

This would devastate his parents. "He's got a wife and son, I doubt he's a flight risk."

Palmer thought for a minute. "Let me see what I can do once I get back to the station."

I stood up and hugged him—awkwardly, because he was still sitting. "You're the best boyfriend ever."

He stood up without letting go of me and looked into my eyes. "You deserve the best," he said.

My heart fluttered and my knees felt weak. I tilted my chin higher to kiss him, and there was a knock at the door. I let go of him and took a step back. "Yes?"

Mackenzie opened the door. "Sorry to disturb you, but Mrs. Williams is here and would like her tea."

I sighed. Of course she would. She didn't trust Mackenzie to choose for her. She didn't trust me to choose until she had no choice, so I was probably stuck with the job for a long time. "I'll be right out."

Turning back to Palmer, I blew him a kiss. "Rain check?"

"Absolutely. I'm taking an hour for dinner at eight. Want to meet me somewhere?"

"Yes. The aunts are gone, and I'm fending for myself, so dinner out would be great."

"Meet me at McGinty's?"

I nodded.

Once Palmer left, I pulled the lavender and chamomile jars off the shelves. "You know, Mrs. Williams, I could choose your tea before you came in and then you wouldn't have to spend so much time standing around in the shop."

She shook her head. "I wouldn't dream of it. It's not that I don't trust you to give me good tea, but it never hurts to be certain."

We were getting faster at assembling her tea, because I'd taken to dumping the jars out, one at a time, in a bowl for easier selection. Half an hour later, she had her weekly tea and was out of the shop.

"I don't know how you stand working with her," Mackenzie said.

I rolled my eyes. "I inherited her with the shop. She was really mad at me for a couple weeks and went somewhere else, but she came back."

Mackenzie grinned. "Maybe you should make her mad at you again?"

We put the jars back on the shelves. "I don't think I can accuse her of murder a second time. We're just stuck with her."

SIMPLY IRISISTIBLE

Chapter 3

I was a little early for dinner that night, so I waited outside in the crisp winter air. McGinty's was an Irish pub and restaurant near the police station and Hannah McGinty, the hostess, always put on-duty officers ahead of the line. We'd been eating here a lot over the past month and, as much as I liked it, I couldn't wait for Palmer to get back on the day shift. I felt like I took too much of his time having dinner together when he was supposed to be working.

I had been busy at work and barely had the time to call Mr. S. to confirm Prashad would be looked after, at least while he was still here in Portsmouth. If he was transferred to a prison, I wasn't sure there was much Palmer could do to keep him safe. I hoped it wouldn't come to that.

I saw Palmer walking down the street to meet me and I walked toward him. He grinned and swept me up in a hug. "You are the light of my day," he whispered in my ear.

I closed my eyes and sank into his embrace, reveling in how cherished he made me feel.

"You're not so bad yourself," I said as we separated. I grabbed his hand and started walking toward the restaurant. "I'm starving. Your tart was all I had time for at lunch."

We walked into the restaurant and Hannah, the hostess and daughter of the owner, greeted us. "Detective, Isabella, nice to see you tonight. Let's get you a table." She picked up two menus, although we'd long since memorized it, and scanned the room for a table. "Follow me, please."

We followed her to a small table in the middle of the room. "Here you are, enjoy your meal."

Palmer helped me with my coat and we sat. "Busy this afternoon?"

I rolled my eyes. "Once you left, Mrs. Williams came in, then we had a steady stream of customers until closing time. I didn't have time to make next week's orders or work on any new products. I've got to go in early tomorrow to finish a tincture for a customer."

Palmer picked up a menu. "You couldn't have finished it tonight?"

"No. It's got to sit in an intermediate step overnight before I add the last ingredient."

He set his menu down. "I thought Mackenzie was going to lighten your workload."

I'd already decided what I wanted to eat, so I left my menu on the table. "Me too. Instead, I've got more customers than ever. It's a good problem to have, overall."

Our waitress, Angela, set two glasses of water on our table. She and Hannah were sisters. In fact, almost related. "Good evening. How's my favorite couple tonight?"

I smiled up at her. "Very good, thanks. How about you?"

"Can't complain. It's a busy night and tips are good. What can I get you tonight?"

Palmer handed her our menus. "I'll have the cedar plank salmon."

My mouth watered. The salmon had a whiskey glaze that was to die for. I considered changing my order, but decided I could just take a bite of his instead. "I'll have the barbeque ribs, please."

After she left, it was time to get serious. "How's Prashad?"

Palmer took a sip of his water. "He's as good as can be expected. He's got a cell to himself, and I told Evans to keep an eye on him."

Officer Evans was in charge of the cells during the overnight shift. "Thank you. I appreciate you looking out for him."

"It's the least I can do, your landlord is a good guy. It's a shame . . ." he trailed off.

"Have you spoken to Prashad? You must have when you arrested him. Did he seem guilty to you?" I asked.

"You know better than that. Some of the best criminals excel at looking innocent, and we can't afford to be taken in like that."

I sighed. I knew that, but I needed to help, and I couldn't leave it alone until I was certain I knew what happened. "What can you tell me about the case?"

He looked at his watch. "You must have been busy at work. It's taken you nine hours to ask me for information I'm not supposed to give you."

I gave him a sly grin. "I don't know what happened. Mr. S. didn't even tell me who Prashad was accused of killing." I knew once Palmer started to tell me about the case, he'd tell me everything he knew.

"He's been arrested for killing his boss, Peter Cafferty."

I arched an eyebrow at him, inviting him to continue.

"The murder weapon is a heavy glass award with a surprisingly sharp tip. Prashad won it last year and he kept it on his desk."

"Prints?" I asked.

Palmer shook his head. "Wiped off."

"Sounds circumstantial to me," I observed.

"You'd think. But everyone in the office heard them arguing the night before the murder. Prashad lost his cool and threatened to hurt Cafferty."

That was bad. "And I suppose he's got no alibi, right?"

Palmer shook his head.

Broomsticks! "You know I have to look into this, right?"

"I would expect nothing less."

Before he could say more, Angela brought our food to the table. "Here you go," she said cheerfully. "You two look far too serious—you're not breaking up, are you?"

I shot a look to Palmer, making sure he appeared as unhappy at that thought as I felt. "Absolutely not. Just talking about work."

"His work, I'm sure. I doubt the apothecary would make either of you look so grim. I'll be back in a few minutes to see if you need anything else."

Once she walked off, he continued. "I was thinking, maybe Thea could come in and look at the evidence. Maybe, you know . . ."

He wiggled his fingers at me, and I burst out laughing. After I convinced Palmer that my family was full of witches, he had each of us show him what we could do. Grandma wasn't thrilled, but even she finally gave in and turned my hair from black to gray. He'd been most impressed with Thea's ability to touch an object and pick up thoughts and emotions and even see a little of what was happening around the object. "Do you think she'd ever help out with an investigation?"

"I'm sure she would. Give her a call and ask."

I took a bite of my ribs and closed my eyes. They were as delicious as ever. "Can I ask you a question?"

"Of course. What's up?"

"I don't want this to sound critical, but I don't understand why you always rush to arrest someone. Why can't you investigate more first, then arrest the right person?"

"I can't afford to give anyone the opportunity to run. I get it right a lot of the time. And even when I don't, having someone else arrested can put the real killer at ease, and hopefully he'll let his guard down."

"Okay, but let's say Prashad is innocent. He's been arrested, and isn't that bad? What if he needed a background check or something? An arrest record would be a problem, wouldn't it?"

Palmer shook his head. "If he turns out to be innocent, he can file a form to have the arrest removed from his record. It'll be like it never happened."

"Really? I had no idea."

"It's not something everyone knows, so if he's innocent, I'll make sure to mention it to him."

"Thanks. On to a happier topic—do you have plans for Christmas?" I asked.

"Now that you mention it, I thought maybe your family would like to have dinner at my house." He reached over and took my hand. "I want to make more time for us to spend together, but I can't until Detective Wheeler is back from her family ski vacation."

My eyes sparkled. "Like a real Christmas dinner? I've never had one of those before. Will there be presents too?"

He smiled. "If you want."

Of course I wanted presents. We exchanged presents for Yule, but they were small and meaningful. We'd never had anything even close to the kind of over-the-top, present-filled day our Christian friends had for Christmas. I loved our Yule gifts, but sometimes a girl just wanted a Barbie Dream House. "I'd love presents. And I'll bring you some too. Tell me everything you want."

He chuckled. "That's not how it's supposed to work. We choose gifts we think other people would like. If I just give you a list and you get everything on it, there's no mystery—no wondering what could be in the next box."

I could barely contain my excitement. I could pick things I thought he should have? How many gifts did a woman get for her boyfriend? Two? Twenty? I had no idea. "Excuse me for a minute," I said.

I stood up and went to the hostess's station to ask Hannah. She was confused to see me in the middle of my meal. "Is everything all right?" she asked.

I couldn't stop grinning. "Yes. But I have a question for you. How do I do Christmas?"

She looked at me like I'd just asked the most obvious question in the world. "How do you do Christmas? You've never celebrated Christmas before?"

I shook my head.

"Oh, honey, you're in for a treat." She looked at the crowd of people waiting for a table. "It's too much to talk about now, but how about tomorrow? I can stop by the shop and we'll talk."

"You're fantastic. Thank you. But first, can you tell me how many presents I should get Palmer? Just a guideline. I don't want too few, but I think too many would be bad too."

She thought for a moment. "It all depends. Think of three tonight, and we'll see if you need more when we talk tomorrow."

I nodded and went back to my table.

"Did you just ask Hannah about Christmas?" Palmer asked.

"I did. I need expert guidance, because I want to get this right."

"You need guidance? I need guidance. I've never hosted Christmas before, and I have no idea how I'm going to do it."

"You'll be fine. If nothing else, the food will be amazing. And we'll have presents, so everyone will be happy. But are you sure you want to invite all seven of us? I wouldn't blame you if you wanted to start out smaller, like just me, or me, Thea, and Delia."

Determination lit in his eyes. "Absolutely not. Your family was so good to me at Samhain, I feel I have to return the favor at Christmas. You're all invited, and I'll just have to work it out."

"Yeah. In two weeks."

He blanched and looked at his watch. "I'll get started tomorrow morning."

"It occurs to me this could be a good play on your part. Inviting seven people for Christmas ensures you have plenty of gifts to open."

He put his fork down. "Oh no. You can't all bring gifts. That's not what I wanted. I don't expect—"

I laughed. "Look at how flustered the serious detective gets when I tell him people want to bring him gifts. You'd better not let the bad guys know this, we don't want your secret out." I changed my tone to be more serious. "But I'll tell everyone else not to go overboard on gifts."

I planned to go at least a little overboard with gifts. Christmas seemed to be the perfect time to show him how much he meant to me. Now all I needed to do was figure out what to get a man who could buy just about anything he wanted for himself.

LISA BOUCHARD

Chapter 4

I woke up the next morning to find Portsmouth transformed into a winter wonderland. Four inches of snow fell after I went to sleep, and all the dingy gray snow piled up on the side of the road had a fresh new covering. Trees had snow clinging to their branches, and icicles hung from the eaves of the house next door. I got out of bed and started humming "Rudolph the Red-Nosed Reindeer." Was I getting into the Christmas spirit?

I hadn't decided yet what to get Palmer for Christmas. A cashmere scarf? Maybe a nice watch? They were nice gifts, but not particularly personal. Maybe something for his kitchen? He regularly cooked fancy dishes that required a well-equipped kitchen to pull off, so I wasn't sure there was anything he didn't already have.

I hoped Hannah had better ideas than I did.

Jameson came into the kitchen as I was making tea. "That feeder doesn't give me much to eat. I'm hungry."

I scowled at him. He could use his magic to get as much food out of the feeder, or to open and serve himself canned food, whenever he felt like it. He wanted me to serve him.

"The feeder is set perfectly. You look like you could lose a little weight."

He jumped up on the counter and took a playful swipe at my hand as I poured milk in my tea. "I don't know why you insist on making me feed you. You're more capable than I am in just about every way. Do it yourself."

"Is this how you talk to all your pets?" he asked.

I laughed. "You're the first pet I've ever had, not that I'd call you one to your face. Somehow I suspect the word 'pet' is more of an insult to familiars. But I tell you what. I'll make you a deal."

He purred. "I'm listening."

"I'll feed you one extra can of food tonight if you go to Palmer's house and see what I can get him for Christmas."

Jameson tilted his head. "How do I know what he wants? Do you want me to ask him?"

My eyes widened. "Absolutely not. This has to be a stealth mission. You need to go when he's not home."

I should be used to his making the same kind of noises humans made, but every time he did, it took me by surprise. He huffed. "Fine. But I expect a large can. How many gift ideas do you need?"

I pursed my lips. "I'm not sure. Maybe ten, just to be safe."

He disappeared before my eyes. He knew Palmer was working nights and sleeping for most of the morning, so he could prowl around Palmer's house under a cloaking spell and never get caught.

That task crossed off my list, I took my tea into the bedroom and got ready for work. I needed to be in early, because Mr. Rojas would be in this afternoon for his anti-inflammatory tincture, and I hadn't finished making it yet.

The first thing I did when I got to the apothecary was go out to the greenhouse. I needed some fresh rosemary, and I wanted to spend a little time with the plants. Maybe I should get Palmer a plant for Christmas. I walked out the back door and was surprised to see a patch of dirt with footprints all around it, as though someone had set up a tent before the snow started falling.

I wondered if it was Alex, the homeless man who had found Hester's body. There was no one besides me in the courtyard, so I couldn't ask. The first thing I did in the greenhouse was take as deep a breath as I could and soak in the sweet smell of the plants. I inspected the plants and was pleased they were doing so well so far this winter. Better than a plant, I thought, I could make Palmer a living wreath from succulents. They wouldn't require much care, which I thought would be good, since I doubted he had many plants in his house. Even if he did, who couldn't use more plants?

I hurried back into the apothecary to finish my work. Mr. Rojas was an early morning customer, and I didn't want to make him wait. I crushed the rosemary and added it to the tincture base I'd created yesterday. I placed the bottle on my warming plate and set the timer for thirty minutes. Once the timer went off, all I had to do was strain it, infuse it with my will, and package it up.

Mackenzie came in at ten, just as I was screwing the top of the tincture bottle closed. "I forgot to take petty cash last night," she said by way of excuse for not having coffee and pastries with her.

I'd forbidden her from using her own money because I didn't think it was fair—I was the boss, and I paid for breakfast. "No problem. I'll go get it. Do you want the usual?"

She took her coat off. "Nah, surprise me."

I grabbed my coat and headed out. While I'd been working, I thought about Alex and how he managed to live outdoors in the winter. I wanted to walk around the block and see if I could find him. If he wasn't around, I'd spend more time looking for him on my day off.

It turns out I didn't have to look far for him. He was set up in the alley across the street from the apothecary. I approached him slowly. "Good morning. I don't know if you remember me, my name is Isabella. You found a woman on the steps of my shop a couple months ago."

He looked up from the book he was reading. After a moment, he seemed to recognize me. "Of course I do. You don't forget a day like that, do you?"

"No, I suppose you don't." Now that I was here, I felt awkward asking him what seemed like personal questions. I decided to press on anyway. "I was wondering, did you set up a tent next to my greenhouse last night?"

Fear crossed his face and I smiled, hoping to put him at ease.

"It's okay if you did, you're welcome to stay there anytime. I just wondered. And honestly, I'm worried about you. It was very cold last night and . . ." I trailed off, not knowing what else to say.

"That was me. But you don't have to worry." He pointed to the sleeping bag strapped to his backpack. "My bag is good to minus thirty degrees. There's nothing New Hampshire can throw at me that I can't take."

"Isn't there somewhere you can go to be warm?" I asked.

"Between the tent and sleeping bag, I'm plenty warm at night. Honestly, I'm colder during the day when I'm up and around."

I shifted my weight from one foot to the other. "Can I help? I don't have a lot of money, but I could give you some. And you can always come into the shop for hot tea if you're cold."

He stood up from the three-legged camp chair he was sitting on. "That's very kind of you. Maybe I'll stop in one day, but I'm just fine. I've been living outside—or 'no fixed abode,' as the police call it—for ten years now, and I don't think I've ever felt better. There's something to be said for being in harmony with the seasons, and staying indoors in artificially heated and cooled air ruins that."

That was a very Wiccan philosophy, and I told him so.

"In that case, would you like to join me for coffee and a pastry? I'm going to the Fancy Tart."

He folded his chair, strapped it to his backpack, then slipped the pack onto his shoulders. "I'm not a charity case."

"I wouldn't dream of treating you like one."

We caught several stares as we walked to the bakery, but I ignored them as we made small talk about the weather.

Once we'd ordered, I asked Alex if he'd prefer to eat inside or outside.

"Inside," he said, looking disapprovingly at my coat that wasn't really warm enough for the day. "You don't look like you're dressed for the weather."

He was right. The walk to work was windier than I'd expected.

"What happened to the woman I found on your doorstep? I never did find out."

It was a long and fairly unbelievable story, and I wasn't sure what I could tell him. "I'm not entirely sure myself. Detective Palmer told me there was no personal connection between her and the murderers."

He frowned. "That's horribly violent for a crime of opportunity."

"It sure is. The killers were caught and are in prison, so we don't have to worry about them anymore."

He stared at me for a moment. "You remind me of my wife. She had the same combination of caring for others while letting bad people be brought to justice as you do."

I smiled. "Thank you." It seemed like an accurate compliment.

"Where is your wife now?" I asked.

"We split up a long time ago. It was better for her if I wasn't around."

That seemed so sad. "I'm sorry to hear that. And I'm not sure if I believe you either. You seem like a perfectly nice person to be around."

He stood and slung his backpack over one shoulder. "You're kind to say that. It's been nice to chat with you, but I've got to go."

I was surprised. I didn't expect he had anything to do with his days, which seemed like a bad assumption on my part. "Of course. Have a good day."

I threw away my trash and headed back to the apothecary with Mackenzie's breakfast. I was pleased to see Hannah waiting for me.

"Are you ready to talk about Christmas?" she asked me.

I grinned. "Absolutely! Let's talk in my office."

"Thanks for breakfast, boss," Mackenzie said as I handed her the white paper bag with a raspberry Danish in it.

I closed the door to my office, because I felt a little awkward not knowing anything about this major holiday, and I didn't want Mackenzie to know. Silly, sure, but who ever said feelings were always rational?

"I did some research this morning and I have some ideas." There was no need to tell her that by research I meant sending my familiar to snoop around his house. "He could use a nicer watch, so I thought that would be good. Other than that, there's nothing he needs, so I decided to go with things I thought he'd like. A coffee bean subscription and a mug that says 'Yoda best boyfriend' with a super cute Grogu and heart on it."

Hannah didn't look sold on my second idea. "Coffee, sure, but the mug? I don't know about that."

"Oh no, it's perfect. I just made him sit through two seasons of *The Mandalorian*."

"How about something romantic?" Hannah suggested.

Jameson hadn't given me any romantic suggestions. Maybe cats don't do romance? "I don't know about that. My whole family will be there, and I don't want them to see anything too personal."

"I like the watch idea. But it has to be a nicer one than he already has. How much are you willing to spend?"

I hadn't factored cost into my shopping ideas. I'd just been happy to have three items to talk about today. "Uh . . . the shop is doing well, but I don't want to spend all my savings on one holiday."

"There are a lot of gifts you can choose that are more thoughtful than hat and scarf, but won't be too expensive. I'm going shopping on my day off, do you want to come with me? Maybe it would be easier to pick things out with a friend."

I smiled at her. "I'd love that. When?"

"I'm going to the Kittery outlets on Friday. They should be fairly empty that morning, so we can get everything we need in one day."

Hannah looked at her watch. "Oh shoot, I've got to run. I'll pick you up here on Friday at eight thirty."

SIMPLY IRISISTIBLE

Chapter 5

Sorority members didn't usually meet, and often didn't know the identities of the other members. I'd asked Hope about this before our first meeting, and she said we needed to start working together, or the fraternity would be able to pick us off one by one.

The sorority had an unhackable method of meeting where we never even had to leave our houses. Each witch had an eight-person dining table in her home and had an assigned seat for meetings, leaving one empty. Tonight there would be two empty seats, and that worried me. I didn't think the fraternity would take it easy on us because we weren't at full strength. Once the meeting started, each witch appeared in their assigned seat at each other witch's table.

Everyone had a large dining table but me, that is. My apartment could only fit a four-person table, so I had to buy a folding card table and chairs to make up the difference. I set my tea mug on the card table and took my assigned seat. The alarm on my phone hadn't gone off yet, so I was still a few minutes early.

This was my second meeting with the sorority, and I hoped it would go better than the first. During the first meeting, several members expressed their disappointment when they saw me. They knew I was a younger witch, but I guess seeing me—or at least the image of me sitting in their dining room—drove home the point that I wasn't just young for a witch. I was really young. The other witches were substantially older than me, although they didn't look much older than my mother.

Hope was our leader because she was the oldest in the group and had the most experience. Eunice had been her second-in-command, but that job now fell to Christina. We all lived in different towns throughout the state. Hope lived in Sewall, Anna lived in Hanover, Sasha lived in Ossipee, Christina was in Keene, and Claire was in Concord.

"Jameson, it's almost time," I called.

He jumped up on the table and sat next to me. "I hate these meetings. You witches take forever to come to decisions about things, and we familiars have to sit and listen to you going back and forth over every little detail."

I wasn't sure that was true. The only other meeting I'd gone to had been short and felt like a job interview. At the end of the meeting, each witch had a list of tasks except me. Christina said I should attend more meetings and get more experience before I started taking on any responsibilities. Her condescending tone, along with my sitting at a card table like a kid at a holiday dinner, made me feel inadequate.

My alarm chimed, and I knew I had one minute to join the meeting. I needed to gain these women's trust and being late would not help. I took a sip of tea and grasped my amulet. I closed my eyes and recited the incantation to join the meeting.

Time to meet to protect our land,

Grant us power to see each other

And make a plan.

My family wasn't into incantations. We tended to put our will into one word or command, at the spur of the moment. Incantations like this one, that didn't even rhyme properly, seemed too stodgy and old fashioned to me. As the literal new kid, I wasn't going to mess around with it though.

I opened my eyes and saw five other witches sitting around my tables. I couldn't believe I was the last one here again. I needed to set my alarm a few minutes earlier.

Jameson yawned and lay down on the table, making his opinion of the meeting clear.

We all looked at Hope, who sat at the head of the table. Her long, curly gray hair was pulled back in a ponytail. She had a notebook in front of her and looked like she was ready for business. Her raven was perched on the back of her chair, preening its feathers. "Good. Now that we're all here, we can begin. Anna, how is your prison initiative going?"

Anna put her toy poodle down on the floor and faced the table. "It's going well. I'm leaving it to each sorority to prioritize locations in their state, but stressing our end-of-the-year deadline. Two states, Vermont and Hawaii, are already done warding their prisons to prevent escape by fraternity members. I expect most will meet our deadline, with California and Texas asking for extensions because of their size."

"Any chance of taking this initiative international?" Christina asked.

"Once we get it wrapped up here, I'm planning to meet with my European counterparts and get them up to speed with everything we've learned," Anna said.

"Good. Keep us informed of your progress. Christina, have you found Forster?"

Christina, a blonde woman with sparkling blue eyes and a deceptively kind smile, spat out a curse. "I can't find him anywhere. I've reached out to other sorority chapters and no one's seen him. No one's even felt him hiding anywhere." The mouse, her familiar, walked up her arm and sat on her shoulder.

Hope frowned. "This is not good news, ladies. What about internationally?"

"I was waiting on the last of the domestic sororities to get back to me before I expanded the search. I'll start contacting them tomorrow."

"Good," Hope said. "Moving on to Sasha. You haven't blown up any more buildings, have you?"

Sasha's crow cawed from somewhere in the room she was in, and Sasha laughed. "Luckily, no. I've got the amulet-making process contained enough that the stone may shatter and leave a scorch mark, but that's it."

I'd planned to listen quietly to the meeting, but I couldn't let this go. "Excuse me, what? You blew up a building?"

Sasha looked at me. "Only one, and it was out in the woods, so no one noticed. Making new amulets is almost impossible without the original incantations. As I said, I've got the process down to just scorch marks now. No usable amulets, but no more property destruction either."

"Good work. You're making real progress, and I have faith you'll have a workable amulet in the next year or so," Hope said.

"Christina and Claire, you already sent me a detailed report about your search for more fraternity members, thank you. Can you bring everyone else up to speed briefly?"

Christina set her wine glass down. "I've been working with my contacts statewide and, so far, everyone we have under observation is leading what looks like a normal, mundane life. They're not meeting, they're not communicating in any way we can detect, and they're not breaking any laws, so I can't get the police involved."

"I'm hearing the same thing from witches watching other fraternity strongholds in the country," Claire said.

Had our capture of Dean and Wayne Cook ruined their plans so thoroughly that they had to go to ground? I didn't think so—they were too committed to their plans to give up. They must be plotting something big, in a way we couldn't see.

"I wouldn't count them out. They're not going to let my family keep them from their goals," I said.

Every witch at the table turned and looked at me like I was an idiot. "We weren't planning to," Hope said kindly, to take away the sting of the glares being shot at me. "Isabella, how is the kitten training going?"

How was the kitten training going? I had no idea. I looked to Jameson. "The kittens are doing fine. In six months, they'll be ready to move to their permanent home."

I relayed the message, since it would have taken too much energy for him to address the other five witches. Claire smiled. "Excellent. I know I shouldn't assume I'll be getting one, but I've already got an amulet, so I should."

I bit my lip. It hadn't occurred to me that the kittens might be split up and go to two different homes. It made sense that one would go to Claire, and the other would choose the last witch of the sorority, as Jameson had chosen me.

"The kittens will choose, correct?" I asked.

"Yes. I hope your family isn't getting too attached to them. Familiars rarely stay with their first family," Hope said.

Thea and Delia would be crushed. It was obvious they'd fallen in love with Jules and Jessamin. "Understood."

"Is there any new business?" Christina asked.

"I have a witch named Helen I'm considering bringing into the sorority, so we would be full again," Hope said.

Christina flicked her eyes to me, then turned to Hope. "I presume you've done a thorough job vetting this witch, and that she's qualified to wear Eunice's amulet."

Jameson's ears flattened almost imperceptibly.

"I have an idea for speeding up our recruitment efforts," Sasha said.

Hope raised an eyebrow. "I thought you said you hadn't been able to make more amulets."

"Not yet, but if each witch needs thorough training before she becomes a member, we could start the training before I perfected my technique, so that as soon as I had more amulets, they'd be ready to take them."

Sasha had emphasized "thorough training," and I tried not to take it personally, but I failed. Jameson's fur raised as he listened to her as well. I'd come a long way in my training and had met every challenge Jameson set for me. I'd also caught my fair share of murderers, both witch and non-witch. I had a lot to be proud of, but apparently Sasha didn't see it that way.

Jameson rested his paw on my hand. "You're doing well, don't listen to them."

"So each witch would share her amulet with another? I can't imagine that going well," Christina said. "Mine has a fit when I take it off just to shower. I don't know what it would do if I tried to have someone else wear it."

"I'm not sure that would work," I said. So much for sitting quietly and just listening for a few meetings. "Brent Thompson tried to put my amulet on, and it screeched in the ears of every witch in the area. It wouldn't allow the chain to go over his head and he had to shove it in his pocket as he tried to run off."

Claire gaped at me. "You let your amulet get stolen?" She looked to the rest of the women at the table. "Tell me again why we allowed her to join us?"

"That's enough, Claire," Hope said sharply.

"That may have been a different situation. If we encouraged the amulets to accept a second witch, they might," Sasha said.

Hope shook her head. "I don't like the idea. We'd be promising witches more power, and if it turns out we can't make more amulets, what would we do? Do you want to share yours for the rest of your life? I know I don't."

The other witches shook their heads.

"What if we trained other witches to combat the fraternity without amulets?" Anna asked.

"They'd be like lambs to the slaughter. I can't ask them to sacrifice themselves like that," Hope said. "No, we need to wait for Sasha to perfect her technique. Until then, it's the six of us keeping the fraternity in check."

My stomach dropped. I'd never realized how important it was to be a member of the sorority.

SIMPLY IRISISTIBLE

Chapter 6

As soon as the meeting wrapped up, Jameson and I left for Proctor House. A cold wind whipped through my hair and had me wishing I'd worn my heavier coat for the walk.

I could have called for a ride, but I wanted to think about the meeting before I filled my family in. They were not going to like the fact no one thought the kittens should stay in Portsmouth or with the family. I doubted the kittens wanted to move either.

"If you're going to walk this slowly, I'll meet you at the house. My paws don't like the snow," Jameson said.

I turned to him just in time to see him vanish. He was lucky there was no one around to notice his disappearing act, but a black cat on a dark night wasn't very noticeable.

Even worse than both kittens leaving town, what would happen if one stayed and the other left? One cousin would be distraught, and rightfully so, thinking they had less power as a witch and they didn't compare to their other cousins.

"Oh broomsticks," I whispered as I stopped walking. Is that what Thea and Delia already thought when they compared themselves to me?

Icy wind blew my hood off, and I started walking again. How had this never occurred to me before?

Jameson was waiting for me in the kitchen of Proctor House. "They're decorating for Yule in the living room, waiting for you."

I smiled. Yule was next week and then Christmas. It was going to be a good week for all of us. The kitchen already had ivy along the tile backsplashes and candles set among branches of mistletoe and holly on the table.

"There you are," Aunt Nadia said as I walked into the living room and kissed my mother. "Your boyfriend stopped by earlier this evening and invited the family to his house for Christmas."

I moved a wreath from the couch to the coffee table and sat down. The room looked like evergreens had taken over, along with mistletoe, birch, ivy, and holly. "Did you cut all this today?" I asked Grandma.

"A little yesterday too," my mother said.

I loved how the house looked during the holidays, and Yule was my favorite. We spent so much time indoors in the winter that it was refreshing to bring more nature into the house. "I tried to talk Palmer out of inviting everyone, saying all seven of us was a lot to handle, but he insisted."

"He's starting to grow on me," Grandma said.

I was amazed. My cousins and I had never dated much, but Grandma had never liked any guy we brought home. "Starting to grow on me" was a huge compliment from her. "Thanks, I like him too."

"How was your meeting with the sorority?" Thea asked.

I handed Grandma some pine branches for the hearth decorations. "Not bad. Claire was her usual self, questioning why I was allowed to have an amulet. By the next meeting, I swear she's going to say it should belong to a stronger witch."

"She's an ornery one," Grandma said. "Can't tell you the number of times Hope has complained about her."

"There was only one other snarky comment, and I'm pretty sure Hope stood up for me once."

Jules and Jessamin ran into the living room, jumping from chair to couch to table, meowing loudly. They collided in midair and fell to the coffee table, knocking a bowl of acorns to the floor.

"Hey!" Delia yelled. "What did we tell you kittens about tearing through our work areas?"

They continued to wrestle with each other, oblivious to the mess they were making, and to the seven women staring at them.

Jameson let out a hiss and they stopped moving.

"What are the rules about roughhousing where the witches are working?"

Jules meowed.

"That's right. There's no running," Delia said.

Thea scratched between Jessamin's ears. "And no squabbling. Now be good kittens and play somewhere else."

They walked off, but as soon as they got into the hallway we could hear them running again. "It's as bad as raising toddlers," Grandma said. "Can't tell you girls the number of times you knocked over half-finished potions or interrupted complicated chants with demands for snacks."

"At least we grew out of it," I said.

Grandma glowered at me as if to say she wasn't convinced that was true.

"Did they say anything about us keeping the kittens?" Delia asked.

I was afraid she was going to ask, and I didn't want to tell her the truth, but finding out later would only upset her more. "They said the kittens would go to other witches in New Hampshire. Claire wants one, of course, but Hope said the kittens will choose who they go to."

Thea's face fell. "That doesn't seem fair. We've put in a lot of work raising them."

Aunt Lily put her arm around Thea's shoulder. "The kittens haven't chosen yet. You've still got time."

"Time for what? There's no way Delia and I will get into the sorority, and by the time they initiate their seventh member, they'll need two familiars. It's hopeless," Thea said as she slumped into a chair.

Jameson hopped into Thea's lap and began to purr. She pet him. "I know we'll have you, but it's not the same. You're Isabella's familiar."

Jameson took the energy to speak to everyone in the room. "The sorority didn't touch on a very important topic—rescuing my family. Do you think Jessamin and Jules will want to work for witches who have abandoned their mother and siblings?"

"No . . ." I said, not sure where he was going with this.

"I can explain this to the kittens, tell them the only way to save their family is to force the sorority to help us rescue them."

"Can the kittens do that?" Delia asked.

"By the time I'm done training them, they'll be able to," Jameson said.

Thea's eyes lit up. "Really? That's great. What kind of rescue operation are we talking about? It took you days to just get these two."

"I don't think it matters," my mother said. "Jameson, how many of your family members does the fraternity have?"

"All of them," Jameson said.

I could tell Thea wanted a number, to see if she'd have a chance to get her own familiar. "More than the sorority can use, right?" I asked Jameson.

"Three sisters, two brothers, and more kittens. I doubt the fraternity has kidnapped only one family, so I can't say for sure how many, or even what kind of familiars they have."

Aunt Nadia crouched next to Jameson. "I'm sorry. We need to rescue your family."

"Is it strange that I already think of them as family? We need to come up with a plan," Thea said.

Grandma put the rest of the pine branches back on the coffee table. "You girls decorate. I'm going to call Hope and get this sorted out."

"I've been thinking about telling Palmer everything about the sorority," I said after Grandma left the room.

My mother pursed her lips in thought. "I agree that at some point he'll need to know, but he has a lot to acclimate to with us, and I don't want to risk telling him too much all at once."

Delia picked up the bowl off the floor and started to put the acorns strewn across the floor into it. "I agree. We should give the poor guy a break. Maybe tell him after Christmas, or after New Year's. Maybe later."

"Unless we need him for something," my mother added.

"We're going to need his help for the rescue operation. Police will make a good distraction when we're ready," Jameson said.

"I already told him a little, and I think he's ready for the whole story. And if we're going to need his help, I don't want to take the time to explain everything then," I said.

"To go back to keeping the kittens, I want them to stay close as well. In fact, I want my entire family close by, living with strong witches, for protection," Jameson said.

I wanted to say something to my cousins about me being the only one with a familiar, but I didn't know what to say. I didn't want to have the conversation in front of the aunts, because they'd probably butt in, and I wanted my cousins to tell me the truth about how they felt.

Grandma returned from her phone call. "Hope says that while it's up to the kittens, they're going to choose based on what's best for the sorority."

Thea and Delia both seemed to deflate. "That's it, then. They'll finish their training and head off to someone else."

Jameson hissed loudly to get our attention. "Not necessarily. We've got months to make the two of you what's best for the sorority. It will be hard work, but we could do it."

I wasn't sure that was true. "But there's only one amulet available. Even if Thea and Delia were ready, only one of them could join the sorority, right?"

Jameson switched to speaking only to me. "We'll have to hope Sasha is able to make more between now and then."

"What did he just say?" Thea asked.

I wasn't sure what to tell her. I didn't want to set up a competition between my cousins. "He's working on a plan to get you both into the sorority."

Delia bit her lip. "I'm not sure I want to join. Can't I just have Jules instead?"

Jules rubbed her head against Delia's ankles and meowed. I wished I knew what she was saying.

"Jules says no," Delia said as she bent down to pet the cat. "She's an all-or-nothing kind of cat."

Grandma groaned. "If it means that much to you, I'll get you a cat, but I don't want to lose any more of my granddaughters to the sorority."

I was confused. "What do you mean? You haven't lost me."

She looked to me with tears in her eyes. "Not yet I haven't. But sooner or later, you're going to run across something you can't handle, just like Eunice."

Eunice was arrogant, though. She thought she could handle anything that came her way, even without a familiar to keep her safe. "I'm not like Eunice, and I have Jameson. And Thea and Delia will have Jules and Jessamin. All the other sorority members are old, Grandma, they were able to evade danger, just like we will."

"If that's the case, then I'm in," Delia said.

Grandma turned and walked away, muttering about the foolishness of young witches these days.

"Really?" I said. It would be nice to have my cousins with me because we made a great team.

SIMPLY IRISISTIBLE

Chapter 7

My phone started playing the theme from *True Detective*. I connected the call. "What's the matter? Run out of bad guys to chase?"

Palmer chuckled. "No, but there's no one at the station right now. Do you know if Thea is busy right now?"

"Hang on, I'll ask." I turned to Thea. "How do you feel about touching some evidence that might exonerate my landlord's son?"

"Your what? Who? I mean . . . of course I'll do it. But you have to explain what's going on. I didn't even know he had a son."

I sighed. "Palmer arrested him for killing his boss and Mr. S. has begged me to help."

Thea put down the candles she had been arranging around the room. "I'll get my coat."

"Grab mine too!" Delia called after Thea as she ran up the stairs to the bedrooms.

Thea was down in a minute with coats, hats, and scarves for herself and Delia. "Ready? Let's go," she said eagerly.

Delia took her coat. "What's up with you?"

Thea was grinning. "It's finally my turn. Let's go."

On the drive to the station, I worked up the courage to ask my cousins a question. "If you two don't get to keep the kittens, will you resent me for having Jameson?"

Delia was driving, so Thea turned from the passenger seat to look at me. "What are you talking about?"

"I was thinking on the walk to the house that maybe you two weren't happy that Jameson picked me and not one of you."

"Are you kidding me? Why wouldn't we be happy for you?" Delia asked.

I sighed. "Because we're all the same. Raised in the same house, have the same amount of power, why would he choose me over one of you?"

Thea laughed. "It's obvious. You're more independent and willing to take risks."

"Am I?"

"Of course you are. You're the one with crazy schemes that we follow along with. And let's face it, you're the only one who keeps finding dead bodies."

I sighed. Yeah, that seemed true. Although, I hadn't found the victim in our current investigation, and that made a nice change. "I didn't find Prashad's boss, though. Maybe my luck is changing."

We pulled into the parking lot of the police station. "So, you're sure you're not upset or anything?"

Delia turned the car off and looked at me. "Nah. And, if we ramp up our training to try and keep the kittens, you should be jealous of us. Jules and Jessamin are so much nicer than Jameson is."

I smiled. "Don't think I hadn't noticed. I'm already jealous of that."

Palmer met us at the door. "Thanks for coming in so fast. I'm not sure how long we'll be alone, so let's get right to it."

We followed him to the evidence room. "Civilians aren't allowed in here, so wait in the hall and I'll bring the murder weapon out."

He unlocked the door and was back out in just a moment. "I want to keep fingerprints off the weapon. Can you get anything if you touch it through the evidence bag?"

Thea knit her brows together. "I don't know. Let me try."

The murder weapon was a heavy glass award with seven sides and a pointed top that looked like it would do a lot of damage to someone. It had, in fact.

Thea took her hand off the bag. "I'm not getting anything."

"Try here," Palmer said, indicating a spot where the bag was touching the glass.

Thea rested her hand on the spot Palmer pointed to and closed her eyes. After a full minute, she took her hand off the bag. "I'm sorry. Nothing. Is it possible to touch the object itself? I've only been able to get readings from touching an actual object."

Palmer turned the award around in his hand. "Does it matter where you touch it? I mean, is one spot better than any other?"

Thea bit her lip. "I don't know. How much trouble would there be, if I left a little partial print or two?"

"Best to avoid that completely," Palmer said. "It would be difficult to explain how they got there if it was dusted a second time for prints."

Delia pointed to the tip of the award. "How about there? You're not likely to leave a readable print if you're gentle."

Palmer handed the bag to me. "Hold this for a second."

I took the bag and examined the award. "I expected there'd be blood on it. Are you sure this is the murder weapon?"

Palmer pulled on a pair of gloves. "After it was printed, the lab washed and collected all the blood for analysis."

That made sense.

"If you open the bag, I'll take it out and Thea can touch it," Palmer said.

Palmer held the heavy glass award and Thea gently touched the sharp, pointed top. She pulled her finger back immediately and stepped away.

Delia put her arm around Thea. "Are you okay?"

Thea nodded. "The emotions were strong, that's all."

Palmer put the award back in the bag. I sealed it and handed it back to him. "Let's put it back before anyone sees what we're doing."

"I'll put it away and I'll meet you in the conference room," he said.

I closed my eyes. I didn't like the conference room, because it brought up memories I'd rather not have. Before I knew I could trust Palmer, he said he knew my family had a secret, and he vowed to find out what it was. In desperation, I followed Jameson's advice and told him. Then I made him forget. The whole process took less than a minute in the conference room, but my conscience had taken a hit that day. I still didn't know how to resolve the problem. Erasing any part of his memory seemed like such a violation of his mind that I wasn't sure I could ever confess what I'd done.

We weaved our way through the desks of the empty office to the conference room and waited for him.

Thea sat and closed her eyes.

"Are you sure you're okay? Can I get you something to drink?" Delia asked.

Thea put her hand on Delia's. "No. Not now. Once we get home I'll have a shot of Grandma's whiskey, or two, and I'll be fine."

Delia sat next to Thea. "I'm taking you home as soon as we're done here."

I sat on Thea's other side. "I'm sorry that was so hard on you. If you don't need me, I want to stay, maybe talk to Prashad for a few minutes."

Thea looked to me. "I'll be okay once I get home, and I'll be much better after you find the person who did this."

Palmer walked into the room, a glass of water in his hand. "You looked like you needed something stronger, but this is all I've got here."

Thea took the glass. "Thanks."

Palmer sat next to me and pulled a notebook out of his pocket. "When you're ready, please let me know what you saw. You can take your time, the most important thing is to be thorough."

Thea nodded and took a sip of her water. "I saw everything from the murderer's point of view. What was the victim's name?"

"Peter Cafferty," Palmer answered.

"Okay. Ah, Peter was in an office. He looked annoyed at the person who was about to murder him."

"Do you have any sense why he was annoyed?" Palmer asked.

Thea closed her eyes for a moment. "Nothing concrete. I don't hear thoughts, but he was annoyed."

Palmer nodded. "Go on."

"The person left the room, and when they returned, Peter turned around, saw the murderer, and started laughing. The person came back and smashed him over the head."

"He didn't try to defend himself?" I asked.

"No . . . he was laughing at the person. He must not have thought they were any kind of threat. They were able to get close to him and he didn't realize he was in any danger until it was too late."

Thea had started to cry. "The poor man. After the first blow, he looked astonished, but couldn't raise his arms or defend himself."

I looked to Palmer as he stood up. "That's all we need," he said. "I'm sorry this has been so upsetting for you."

"I'll take her home," Delia said.

Palmer and I walked my cousins out of the building. I hugged Thea tightly before she got into the car. "I'm sorry. I'll make it up to you somehow."

After they left, I turned to Palmer. "I'd like to talk to Prashad, let him know I'm looking into the case."

Palmer took my hand in his. "It's not looking good for him. I'd hoped Thea would be able to see who the murderer was. Without some evidence pointing to another suspect, I'm afraid he's going to be convicted."

I bit my lip. The family man I'd seen when I'd followed Mr. Subramanian didn't look like a murderer. He had too much going for him. "I'm not going to tell him that, though."

My phone chimed. I pulled it out of my pocket to see the alarm message. "And then I've got to go."

Palmer frowned. "Where are you going so late at night?"

I made a goofy face. "Sorority business at midnight."

Prashad was still being held in a cell at the police station, so Palmer walked me to an interrogation room. "Wait here and I'll bring him to you. I have to listen to everything he says, so you need to tell him that."

I nodded and sat at the interrogation table, happy to be on the side that didn't have a bar to attach handcuffs to.

Minutes later, Palmer opened the door. "Have a seat." He closed the door on us and Prashad sat at the table.

I smiled at him, hoping to put him at ease. His face was drawn and he had dark bags under his eyes. "Hi, Prashad. We've never met, but your father has asked me to look into your case."

"My father?" he asked.

"I'm Isabella Proctor, I'm one of his tenants. Before we start talking, I'm not the police, but Detective Palmer is listening in behind the mirror. Don't incriminate yourself."

He furrowed his brow. "Why are you talking to me?"

"I promised your father. He asked me because he knew I was close to Detective Palmer."

His eyes widened. "He's pinning my freedom on the fact that you're dating the man who arrested me?" He stood up and paced the room. "I need my lawyer. Can you get him here this late at night?"

"I don't know. I just wanted to let you know you're not alone and that we're working to try and get you out."

"Great. Fine, whatever."

Palmer opened the door. "Let's get you back to the cell." He looked to me. "Isabella, I'll meet you at my desk."

I went back to his desk and sat. Palmer's desk had been tidied recently. There were no loose papers or files sitting on it, and even the pens were standing neatly in their holder.

I didn't blame Prashad for being harsh with me. I didn't want to explain my background in solving murders, so to him I was exactly what he said—the girlfriend of the man who arrested him. I should have Mr. S. tell him more about me.

Palmer arrived and sat next to me. "I'm sorry about that. He shouldn't have been so rude to you."

I put my hand on his arm. "It's okay. He's falling apart in here. At the very least, he needs to get out on bail, be home with his family."

The alarm went off on my phone.

"Do you have time to talk to the victim's wife before you need to go home?"

It was eight o'clock. I didn't need to meet the coven until midnight. "I've got two hours, that's it." I had four hours, but I wanted to make sure I wasn't late, and this would give me some time to think before the meeting.

He beamed. "Plenty of time. Let's go."

LISA BOUCHARD

Chapter 8

Palmer rang the bell of the Cafferty house. I say house, but honestly, it was large enough that it could probably be called a mansion. The entire neighborhood was made up of large houses with expansive lawns. Backyards had pools and tennis courts.

The white door opened and a woman in a black dress glared at us. "Can I help you?"

"I'm Detective Palmer, Portsmouth PD. This is my associate, Isabella Proctor. We're here to speak to Mrs. Cafferty."

The woman's eyes widened. "Oh, sorry. You wouldn't believe how many people have been coming to the house to gawk." She opened the door and stepped aside. "Please, come in. Mindy is in the living room."

"Thank you. And you are?" Palmer asked.

She started walking, and we followed, our shoes clacking on the wood floor. "I'm Bess Higgs. I live next door. Elise and I have been taking care of Mindy these past few days."

She turned to face us. "She's heartbroken, of course, but she can't move on until after the funeral. She's stuck in a horrible waiting period that's adding to her grief. Is there anything you can do to speed up the investigation?"

Palmer used his gentlest tone. "That's why we're here, ma'am. As you can see, we are working day and night on the case and will do our best to find the guilty party as soon as possible."

The corners of her mouth raised in a weak smile. "Thank you. I'm not sure how much longer she can take it."

She led us into the living room, where two women sat on a red leather couch. It was easy to tell which woman was Mrs. Cafferty—her eyes and nose were red from crying. The other woman was more composed. When she turned to look at us, she raised an eyebrow.

"Mindy, the police are here to talk to you," Bess said.

She didn't look away from the fire, and didn't seem to hear anything.

The other woman stood up. "Let's talk in the kitchen."

We followed her through the large formal dining room into the kitchen. She held her hand out for Palmer and me to shake. "I'm Elise Collins, Mindy's best friend. She's not in any state to answer questions right now, so how can I help you?"

"I'm Detective Steve Palmer and this is my associate, Isabella Proctor. There's never a good time for a murder investigation, and yet the sooner we can ask Mrs. Cafferty the questions we have, the sooner we can bring our investigation to a close."

She opened the refrigerator and took three bottles of water out. "Water?"

Palmer declined, so I did as well. I had no idea if there was a protocol for accepting food or drink while questioning people. I'd have to ask him later.

Elise sat at the kitchen island, but didn't invite us to join her. "Let me save you some time. I haven't left her side since this horrible ordeal started, and I've known her since kindergarten. I'm sure I can answer anything you want."

I thought Palmer would tell her no, but instead he pulled a stool out from the kitchen island and sat down. "Thank you, Mrs. Collins. Were the Caffertys happily married?"

Elise shifted in her stool. "I'd say so, yes. At least as happy as any other couple who had been together for decades." She took a sip of her water. "If you ask me, Mindy could have done better for herself, but she didn't listen to my advice back then."

Palmer pursed his lips. "You didn't like Mr. Cafferty?"

She raised her hands. "That's not what I meant. He was a decent guy, never treated Mindy badly, but she could have married someone with more power and influence instead of a corporate manager."

I shook my head. I'd never heard anyone speak about marriage with such a mercenary tone before. "I presume she married him because they fell in love."

She looked past Palmer to me. "You're too young to understand. Love doesn't get your kids into the Ivy League. Love doesn't buy a country club membership, or private school, or anything worth having."

Yikes! I felt bad for her husband.

Palmer cleared his throat. "What do you know about Mr. Cafferty's morning routine?"

"Nothing. I don't live in the neighborhood," she said.

"That's fine. Have you seen, or has Mrs. Cafferty mentioned, strangers lurking around the neighborhood?"

She stood up and put her water bottle next to the sink. "She hasn't mentioned any, but honestly we're too busy right now to worry about what's going on outside." She sat back down but was still full of nervous energy. "Honestly, if they'd moved to a better neighborhood, with a stronger homeowner's association, the gates would be fixed and people wouldn't be able to roam the streets at will."

Palmer looked concerned. "Were the gates purposely broken, and did anyone report the issue to the police?"

She shrugged. "You'd have to ask Bess. Her husband is on the HOA committee."

Palmer pulled his notebook out and wrote something down. "I'll do that. One final question, if you don't mind. Do you know where Mrs. Cafferty was the morning her husband was murdered?"

Color drained out of her face. "You can't possibly think Mindy had anything to do with his murder. You need to leave. We're done answering your questions."

She stood up and started walking to the front door. We followed, but when we got to the living room, Palmer veered off and sat next to Mrs. Cafferty.

"Ma'am," he said softly. When he had her attention, he continued. "I'm Detective Palmer. I'd like to ask you a few questions."

She stared at him, and I could see the effort she expended to focus on him and what he was saying. Only then did I notice the empty wine bottles on the side table.

She turned to Bess. "Can you get me a cup of coffee?"

Bess stood. "Of course. I'll be right back." She looked to Palmer and me. "Can I get you anything?"

Again, we declined.

Elise Collins stormed into the living room. "I said we were done here and it was time for you to go."

Palmer ignored her. "I know it's difficult to think about, but did your husband have any enemies at work, or in his personal life?"

She wiped a tear away. "I thought you had his . . . found the person who did this already? That man who worked with him, Prashad something."

"He is a suspect, but we want to get a full picture of your husband's life before we charge him. How about anyone closer to home? Anyone in the neighborhood?"

Bess returned with coffee for Mindy and herself. She sat and patted Mindy's knee.

"No one," Mindy said. "We're neighbors, a little community. We wouldn't kill each other."

I sat in an armchair and studied Mindy, wondering if she'd killed her husband and was now putting on a show for us. Her puffy eyes and red nose weren't an act, but was everything else?

"While we're on the subject of your community, has anyone new entered your life? New staff or neighbors? Particularly anyone who didn't feel quite right to you?"

She took a sip of her coffee and looked to Bess. "I can't think of anyone, can you?"

Bess shook her head. "No. You haven't hired anyone new, and I haven't noticed anyone else hanging around."

"Just one more question, if you don't mind," Palmer said.

She took a deep breath. "Of course not. Anything I can do to help."

"Did your husband seem worried or distracted lately?"

"A bit. He was worried about his retirement. He'd chosen his successor, and the rest of his department wasn't happy about it."

She paused for a moment. "But I thought you knew that already. Isn't that why you arrested Prashad? They had a huge fight last week because Prashad thought he deserved the promotion."

"What I don't understand is why he was in the office so early that morning. Do you think he was having an affair with his successor? Maybe that's how she got the job," Elise said.

Palmer nodded. "Did your husband feel like his life was in danger?"

"No. He was more disappointed than anything else. But he shook it off, saying we'd never have to worry about this kind of thing once we got to Arizona."

"You were planning to move?"

She nodded. "I still want to, once the case is closed."

Elise, who was standing in the doorway, said, "I don't think you should make any plans to move just yet. You're under a lot of stress, and I don't think you should make any big decisions right now."

A tear slid down Mindy's cheek, and she reached for a tissue.

Palmer stood up. "Thank you for your time. Please call if you think of anything else I should know."

He handed a business card to each of the women in the room.

We left the living room, but Elise blocked our path in the hallway. "I hope you're happy with yourselves. It's going to take us hours to settle her down again."

"I'm sorry," I said, because it didn't look like Palmer was going to say anything.

She led us outside. "I thought of something once you were talking with her. Bess's husband, Marlon, threatened Peter a few weeks ago. They were arguing about putting up new streetlights. Peter said stay with the burnished copper lights over his dead body, and Marlon said that could be arranged." She shuddered. "Do you think Marlon could have killed him? Over streetlights?"

"We'll check it out," Palmer said. "Good night."

Once we got into his car, Palmer said, "You were uncharacteristically quiet in there. You okay?"

I nodded. "I wasn't sure how much you wanted me to interrupt you, so I didn't. Besides, you looked like you had it all under control."

He started the car and pulled away from the curb. "You don't have any potion or spell to tell when people are lying, do you?"

I thought for a moment. "There is a spell to compel people to tell the truth, but I can't do it on my own."

"How about potions?"

"None that I know of. I'd never sell anything like that. I can look through Trina's files for one tomorrow."

My phone rang. It was my mother. "Hi, Mom, I'm on my way home now."

"Good," she said. "There's a very unpleasant woman here trying to insist she be allowed to bond with the kittens."

73

I sighed. That must be Claire. "Is Hope there?"

"Not yet. Your grandmother is at her wit's end keeping Claire distracted."

"Okay. I'll be there in a few minutes. Palmer's driving me now."

I hung up.

"Trouble?" he asked.

"No more than usual. There's a witch at the house who thinks she should have one of the kittens for her own. She's trying to make them bond with her."

He scoffed. "I've had cats in the past, and there's no way anyone can make them do something they don't want to. I imagine that goes double for cats that can talk back to you."

"I don't know. I need to get to the house and sort this out, though. We can talk more about the case tomorrow."

He didn't put his flashing lights on, but he still got me to Proctor House in record time. I leaned over and gave him a quick kiss. "Thanks. Maybe some night soon we can get together without having to experiment on evidence or question witnesses."

"I'd like that," he said.

SIMPLY IRISISTIBLE

Chapter 9

I got to Proctor House later than I wanted, but still before midnight. The living room was filled with witches laughing and, judging from the empty glasses on the table, drinking a wide variety of cocktails.

"Isabella, there you are," my mother said.

"I thought you said only Claire was here," I whispered.

"As soon as I hung up, everyone else arrived. Hope read Claire the riot act about forcing a relationship with any sentient being, and she seems suitably chastised. The kittens haven't come out from wherever they're hiding though."

I didn't blame them.

I smiled at her. "You look like you're having fun. Did the liquor come out before or after everyone got here?"

"It was Hope's idea. She felt the tension in the room and this was her suggestion."

I looked past her. "I'm going to check on Thea before we get started. She was shaken up by what she saw tonight."

My mother shook her head. "Don't. She's fast asleep. She asked me to cast a sleeping spell on her for the night."

That had been a good idea. If she had a good night's sleep, she'd be able to deal with any leftover emotions easier tomorrow.

I walked to the bar and poured myself a glass of juice. I wanted a clear head for my first in-person sorority meeting. I looked around the room and recognized everyone but one woman, who I assumed was Helen. She was a short, apple-shaped redhead dressed all in black.

Hope noticed me first and looked at her watch. "Cutting it a bit fine, don't you think?"

I looked at the clock on the wall. Eleven fifteen. It was later than I thought. How long had we been at the Cafferty house?

Hope set her drink down and clapped her hands. "Ladies, we're all here now and I think we can begin."

Grandma and the aunts all stood up. "Thank you for choosing our house for this honor. We'll leave you to your work now," Grandma said.

I frowned and looked at her. An honor? She was anti-sorority, so I didn't understand why she would say that. It wasn't that she didn't approve of what the sorority did or stood for, she'd just spent a lot of time and energy trying to keep her family out of it. She'd done a good job, too, until Mrs. Thompson came into my life and brought me into the sorority after her death.

Maybe Grandma was just being polite because Hope was her friend.

They left the room and then it was just the seven of us.

"Take your seats, ladies," Hope commanded.

I thought we'd have the ceremony outside, but maybe we weren't. We sat on the couches and chairs of the living room and looked expectantly at Hope.

"Today we welcome our sister, Helen, into the Sorority of Brigid. The sorority has stood for more than two hundred years against the darkness."

"Before the sorority was formed, we were women afraid to show our talents. We were right to remain hidden from the ever-present threat of anti-witch hysteria, which still exists today," said Christina.

"Our sorority began when we started banding together in small groups for study and mutual support. We wrote our knowledge in secret grimoires, keeping them hidden to protect ourselves from those who would lash out at us in hatred," said Sasha.

"Witches calling themselves the Fraternity of Free Witches, once our honorable counterpart with the same purpose as our early sorority, departed from our ideology of do no harm in favor of using their talents to gain power. We faced a new evil, within our own community," Christina said.

"Our ancestors strengthened the Sorority of Brigid, created amulets, and redefined our mission to keep the fraternity from achieving their aims. And we are still here, holding the fraternity at bay, even as they increase their numbers," said Hope.

I had heard bits and pieces from Eunice and Jameson, but never such a clear account of the sorority's long history.

"All stand," Sasha said.

We stood and joined hands, with Hope and Helen in the middle of our circle.

Hope continued. "Do you, Helen, freely take on the burden of the Sorority of Brigid? Will you fight to your last breath to keep magic pure and out of the hands of evil?"

"I will," she said.

Hope removed Eunice's amulet from her neck and placed it over Helen's head. I held my breath, because the amulet could reject Helen. I'd seen it happen when Brent tried to wear mine.

Helen smiled with relief. "Thank you."

Hope stepped back to join the circle. "Now we chant the protective spell."

What the what? No one had chanted a protective spell over me when I joined. This was beginning to feel personal. I had no idea what the spell was, so I couldn't say it with everyone else. With any luck, being a second behind wouldn't mess anything up.

"Protector Brigid, protect our sister Helen, and all the sisters in this circle.

"Guardian Brigid, watch over us as we sleep and as we are distracted by our daily lives.

"Wise woman Brigid, give us your wisdom to know the proper path in life.

"Healer Brigid, keep us hale and whole as we battle the forces of evil.

"Mother Brigid, hold us to you, keep us safe, shelter us as only a mother can."

I felt a surge of power race through the circle into each of us and then focus on Helen. The ceremony was over, and I could feel the protective circle break as other witches released their hands. I was holding on to Christina and Anna and never wanted to let go. I wanted this feeling to stay with me.

LISA BOUCHARD

Anna pried her hand out of mine. "It's okay to let go. The power stays with you."

Reluctantly, I released my grasp on both witches. Instantly, the power stopped coursing through me, but I still felt it—a tiny spark deep within me, ready to be called on when I needed it.

One by one, each member of the sorority hugged Helen and welcomed her. I went last, trying to decide what to say. "Welcome, Helen. May your strength and wisdom enrich our sorority."

I hoped that was okay. No one seemed upset or shocked, so I guess it was. "Thank you, Isabella."

The aunts returned with trays of finger food. Of course they did—no one escaped Proctor House without being fed. They set their trays down and left, not saying a word. Almost like they were servants to the sorority. I wasn't sure I liked the feeling of being served by my family.

We sat back down and helped ourselves to the sandwiches, mini quiches, and tiny pastries. Aunt Nadia had gone all out for the sorority, even polishing the silver trays we never used.

"Do you think I'll get a familiar any time soon?" Helen asked.

Claire snorted. "Good luck with that. I haven't had one for a decade. I should have got the next one, but it seemed Beatrice had other plans for him."

I tried, and failed, not to gape at her. She was talking about Jameson. I thought he stayed with the amulet. He told me he came with the amulet, making me feel like I had no choice but to accept him. We were going to have words about this.

It was no wonder he was trying to keep the kittens from Claire. If he hadn't wanted to go to her, it made sense he wouldn't want them to either. I was beginning to wonder about the sorority. I thought we were one cohesive group, at least now that they had accepted me. But had they? Why didn't I have an initiation ceremony?

"Did Mrs. Thompson do something wrong when she chose me? Was she not supposed to give me the amulet and Jameson?" I asked the group.

The other women stopped talking and looked to me. "Usually, a witch has to earn her familiar. They aren't passed along like a family heirloom," Christina said.

"I didn't realize," I said softly. No wonder I wasn't a favorite in the group.

I stood up. I needed to clear the air somehow, or I'd always be the odd witch out in the group. "Hope, could I speak to you privately?"

"Of course, dear. Why don't we go into the kitchen?"

She followed me into the kitchen and closed the door behind her. "We don't need to have everyone else listening in."

We were witches. If another member of the sorority wanted to, I was sure they could cast a spell to hear us. "Yes, well, just in case . . ." I said as I cast a cloaking spell around the two of us.

"What's wrong?" Hope asked.

"I feel like I'm not wanted in the sorority." I began to tick off reasons on my fingers. "I didn't get an initiation. Other members are outright angry about how I got Jameson. It took weeks for you to decide whether to let me in or not, even though I had Jameson and the amulet."

I sighed. "I don't know what to do about it, either. If the fraternity tries anything soon, we can't afford to have the other members not accept me."

Hope sat at the table. "You're right. But if I try to force them to accept you, that will backfire. It all comes down to the kittens. If they choose Claire and Helen, the members' other objections will fade away."

I leaned against the sink. "There's nothing I can do about that. My cousins love those kittens and, from the looks of it, it's mutual."

Hope frowned, but said nothing.

"Is there anything we can do to find more familiars?"

"Honestly, I don't know. When Eunice and Claire lost their familiars, we all assumed more would appear. We didn't know what to make of it when none arrived. This is a question for Jameson. He may have a better idea how an animal becomes a familiar. He's always been reluctant to share that information, though."

Great. I doubted my ability to get secrets out of him. "I'll ask, but don't hold your breath."

"As for your initiation, that's my fault. I didn't want to force your acceptance on anyone. But you should know we are all recommitted to the sorority through each initiation, and the power and protection given to Helen goes to each of us in the circle as well."

That was fine, now. But had they left me relatively unprotected for weeks? I shook my head. It was late and I didn't have the energy to make an issue out of it.

"I'll speak to each of them tonight as soon as you go home. You'll find them much more accepting the next time we meet. I can promise you that."

I took my coat off the rack by the door and put it on. "Okay. I'll talk to Jameson and let you know if he explains anything to me."

I left Proctor House without saying good night to anyone, and walked home in the dark.

LISA BOUCHARD

Chapter 10

I got to the apothecary early the next morning to get a head start on the new potion I was developing—an insomnia potion that helped settle a person's mind before they went to sleep.

I opened the door and went through my daily routine: lit a candle for Trina, started brewing tea—chamomile mint for today—and opened my office.

Through the window, I saw Alex's tent pitched next to the greenhouse. I was glad he took me up on my offer to stay out back.

Before I could make the insomnia potion, I needed to look through Trina's old files for a truth potion. Forcing someone to tell the truth was not a good idea, and I hoped she didn't have one.

After an hour of looking through the files, I was relieved I didn't find one. I could probably create one, but using my magic in this way was a step toward the dark side I wasn't willing to take.

It was time to get to work making potions that helped people. I pulled the insomnia potion ingredients down from the shelves in the prep room and got to work. The potion wasn't quite right yet, so today I was going to gently heat the crocus blossoms in water before adding the other ingredients.

My herbalist intuition told me what remedy each of my customers needed, and it told me when a potion was ready for people to use, but it let me work out how to create the potion on my own. Frustrating? Definitely, but I learned a lot by creating potions on my own.

Once the crocus was warming, I ground the lavender buds and dried purslane leaves with a drop of almond oil. My mind wandered to Prashad. I wasn't sure what else I could do to help him that Palmer wasn't going to do himself. Kate was back from vacation and due to meet up with Palmer this afternoon. Then he'd have her, not me, as a sidekick again.

It wasn't that I was jealous of Kate, it was just that I really liked questioning suspects and solving cases. Honestly, I might like it better than running the apothecary. Don't get me wrong, I loved helping people, but in another year or two, I'd be ready to come in one day a week and make potions, then let someone else manage the store for me.

Mackenzie walked in as I was wrapping up this version of the insomnia potion. It still wasn't right, but it was closer. I could tell because when I tried to infuse it with my intention, the potion would not absorb it. I stored the potion in a labeled bottle and wrote notes in my notebook about what I'd done and what the results were. If I didn't keep notes, kind of like I did in chemistry class, I'd forget and start duplicating my work.

"Good morning," I called to her from the prep room.

"Morning, Isabella," she said as she hung up her coat. "Still working on the insomnia cure?"

Mackenzie was not a witch, so she knew nothing about the real work of making potions. That was fine—she didn't need to know to do her job.

"Yeah, it's not really coming together for me yet. I'll have to think about it more, maybe more research would help too."

Mackenzie made a face. "More research. Sounds too much like school for my taste."

"It's a lot different when you're researching something you really love, though."

The door chime rang and Palmer walked in. He looked like he was having a rough day, and it was only eleven thirty. His hair was mussed, like he'd been running his hands through it in frustration. I smiled at him.

"Good morning, Detective Palmer," Mackenzie said.

He gave her a brief smile. "Morning, Mackenzie."

She made him a mug of tea and handed it to him. "Whatever is wrong, tea can't hurt."

He accepted the mug and turned to me. "Can I speak to you in your office?"

I nodded. Once I closed the door, he took a sip of the tea and sank into a chair.

"What's up?" I asked. I didn't like the deep furrow in his brow.

"You didn't find a potion that will make people tell the truth, did you? I can't crack my suspect. You don't have someone who can read minds, do you?"

I shook my head. "No. I looked, but we don't have anything like that. I don't know anyone who can read minds either. But even if I did, you couldn't possibly use the information in court."

After another sip, he said no. "But if I knew he was telling the truth, I'd start looking for more suspects."

I sat in my chair and thought for a minute. "What would you do before you knew magic existed?"

"I'd go hard on him until he confessed."

I was surprised to hear that. "You would? Even if you have doubts about his guilt?"

Palmer nodded.

"But you have doubts, otherwise you wouldn't be here right now."

He drained his mug and set it on my desk. "Yes. It's hard—once you learn magic is real, you can't go back. I can't help but wonder how it could help me, help the department. If we had someone who could read minds, we could clear so many cases."

I frowned. "Until you have to explain your evidence. I'm not sure there are any witches who want everyone to know about their powers. It's not a very big leap from helping the police question suspects to surveilling people who haven't done anything wrong yet."

He sighed. "I suppose you're right. I shouldn't have pinned my hopes on Thea being able to solve the case right away."

I stood up and put my hand on his shoulder. "Believe me, magic doesn't lead to many shortcuts, it usually makes things more complicated."

He reached up and took my hand. "I know."

"Is there anything else I can do to help?"

He squeezed my hand. "Maybe watch the next interrogation. Are you free right now?"

I thought for a moment. Mackenzie could handle the store on her own and I'd caught up on my potion making. "I am. I'd be happy to watch your interview. But what do you think about me asking him questions and you watching him? People have always opened up to me."

He stood up. "We can give that a try. It can't hurt."

~*~

Prashad and his lawyer were waiting for us in the interrogation room. I sat across the table from them and smiled, trying to put Prashad at ease.

Instead of relaxing, his body went stiff. "I thought you were helping me. Now you're here to question me. You're not even a cop, and I'm not telling you anything."

His lawyer put a hand on his arm to stop him from saying anything else. "John Sweeney. And you are?"

I held my hand out to him. "Isabella Proctor."

He didn't look impressed. "My client tells me you're the detective's girlfriend. Why, exactly, are you here?"

I flushed. "I am. But I'm also your client's father's tenant. Mr. Subramanian asked me to do what I could to protect your client while he was here and to help the police find the real murderer."

Sweeney nodded. "I see." He leaned to whisper in Prashad's ear. Prashad nodded. "My client will cooperate, for now."

I smiled at them both. "Thank you."

"Does he have to be in here too?" Prashad said, looking at Palmer.

"I'm afraid he does. He won't interfere with us, though. Isn't that right, detective?"

Palmer nodded.

"Good. Prashad, your office was very close to the victim's. You must have heard arguments from time to time. I'd like you to list everyone who argued with Mr. Cafferty over the past year."

Prashad's body relaxed. "Who didn't argue with him? Everyone from secretaries to vice presidents. He wasn't a likable guy. But I never heard anyone threaten to kill him."

I leaned back in my chair. "A person who really wanted to harm him probably wouldn't announce it." I turned to Palmer. "Are we checking the alibis of people in the company already?"

Palmer nodded.

"Okay, we've got people on that. Can you tell me why you argued with him the night before he died?"

Prashad looked to his lawyer, who nodded. "I've been doing my job and half his job since he decided to retire a year ago. He promised me—promised me—that he would recommend me to replace him. He didn't. Instead, he promoted Gwen Vandermeer. Gwen doesn't know how to run a department. She can barely run a printer. I suppose it was all the private lunches they had together that convinced Cafferty she should have the job."

"That's terrible. What did you decide to do when you heard the news?" I asked.

"I didn't plan to kill him, that's for sure. That wouldn't even make sense. If I wanted the job, I'd have gone after her, wouldn't I?"

He was right about that. Killing Cafferty wouldn't get him the job he was promised.

"I rewrote my résumé and sent it out to several headhunters. You can check my laptop and email. All I wanted to do was leave and go somewhere that my work was appreciated."

I shifted in my seat. "But your work was appreciated. The murder weapon was a symbol of that."

Sweeney put his hand on Prashad's arm again, and Prashad said nothing.

"If we look at your email, we'll see that your actions after being passed over for promotion were to update your résumé and look for a new job. Is that all?"

Prashad nodded. "You know my parents. Do you think they'd have raised a killer?"

I didn't. The Subramanians had been kind and thoughtful, even when I was responsible for the arson on the building. If I'd had any doubt, I'd never have agreed to help him. "No, that's why I'm here."

"I'll present the necessary documentation from my client's laptop," Sweeney said.

"Thank you," Palmer said.

"Okay then. I've got one more question for you. Where were you early on Friday morning? If we can corroborate your alibi, we might be able to get you out of here."

Prashad looked to his lawyer. "You need to tell them, Prashad. You can't allow your embarrassment to put you in jail."

Prashad closed his eyes and sat back in his chair. "I was trying to exercise," he muttered.

"Thank you for telling me. Were you at a gym?"

"No. I was trying to jog around my block, but it was more of a hobble and limp. I've never been in good shape and wanted to surprise my wife. I'd been getting up early, before she woke up, so she never knew what I was doing."

She couldn't vouch for where he was, because she'd have been sleeping. "Can you think of any neighbors who would have seen you?"

Prashad shook his head. "I didn't see anyone, but no one would have recognized me. I had my hoodie on, and pulled the hood over my head so no one could see my face."

Sweeney interjected. "My client felt awkward about being out of shape and wanted to keep his identity a secret while exercising. Most people join a gym in a town they don't live in for that same reason."

They do? I had no idea. But I knew a thing or two about keeping hidden. "How early in the morning were you out?"

He made a face. "Four thirty. I don't suggest it."

We'll canvas the neighborhood and see if we can find anyone who saw you."

I wasn't sure what else to ask him. "Thank you for being so honest with me. Is there anything else you want to let us know?"

I thought Sweeney would prevent him from speaking, but he didn't. "I didn't kill my boss. I don't feel that kind of rage—ever. I find constructive solutions to my problems, like find a new job."

Sweeney stood up. "I think that's all my client has to say for now."

I shook his hand. "Thank you. We'll look into everything we learned today." I wanted to add that we'd find a way to clear Prashad's name, but I couldn't promise that.

The four of us left the interrogation room. An officer brought Prashad back to the cells, Sweeney left, and Palmer and I went to sit at his desk.

"Did I help?" I asked.

He smiled. "Yes. You got him to give us his alibi. He refused to say where he was that morning. Now we can either clear him or charge him. Good work."

I grinned back at him. "Good. I'm glad."

Kate walked up to us, her tan face letting everyone know she'd been to the Bahamas for her vacation.

"How was your trip?" I asked.

She sighed. "It was fun, but I think I'm getting too old to go on family vacations. My aunt and uncle were great, but it was a lot of together time, not enough time laying on the beach pretending to read a book."

I smiled at her. If my family went on a vacation together, it would be about the same.

"How'd the interrogation go?" Kate asked.

"Excellent. He says he was out at four thirty in the morning. I want you and a couple others to canvas the neighborhood for someone who saw him."

"You got it, boss," she said and then walked away.

"I've got to talk to Marlon Higgs about his alibi. I seem to be short a partner now, want to come along?"

93

LISA BOUCHARD

Chapter 11

The Higgs house was the same design as the Cafferty house, only it was painted sage green. Palmer rang the doorbell, but no one answered. He looked into the garage and came back. "Two cars, so he's probably home."

Palmer banged on the door and it swung open.

"All right already, what?" the man in the barely closed bathrobe said. He winced at the light streaming into his house. I looked closer at him, and he looked like he'd had a rough night. I'd never been hungover, but I imagined if I had, I'd look a lot like Mr. Higgs.

"Mr. Marlon Higgs?" Palmer said, keeping his professionalism intact. "Police. We'd like to ask you a few questions."

Higgs stood up straighter and, thank Brigid, pulled his bathrobe fully closed. "About what?" he asked.

"May we come in?" Palmer asked.

He looked us up and down. "How about some ID first?"

Palmer pulled out his shield. I wanted to shrink into the background so no one would even see me. "Detective Steve Palmer, and special consultant Isabella Proctor."

I tried not to grin like an idiot, but I think I failed. Special consultant was a great title. It could mean anything, but wow, it made me feel good. I put on my serious face, the same one I used when Jameson was scolding me for getting a spell wrong, and I wanted him to think I wasn't internally rolling my eyes for all they were worth.

Higgs looked sufficiently intimidated, which is what Palmer was going for. He opened the door wide and stepped aside. "Of course, please come in."

I followed Palmer and was surprised to see the inside of the house was also exactly the same as the Cafferty house. No individuality, how disappointing.

"I was just making coffee. Can I get you some?" Higgs asked as we followed him to the kitchen.

He had one of those coffee pod machines, so I shook my head. "No, thank you."

Palmer declined as well. "We need to ask you about the altercation you had with Peter Cafferty."

Higgs looked genuinely confused. "Altercation? We never fought."

"Altercation might be too harsh a word. You two argued at a meeting several days ago, and now he's dead."

Palmer pulled a chair out from the kitchen island and sat down, and I followed his lead. We weren't going anywhere until he told us everything.

Higgs put sugar in his coffee and stirred it. "Oh, that. That was nothing. We were arguing about streetlights."

Streetlights? What a weird thing to argue about.

"What about them?" I asked.

Higgs sighed. "Peter wanted to spend half our homeowner's association money to replace them with some god-awful modern chrome design. He wanted to replace the current bulbs with ones so bright it would almost look like day on the streets."

Palmer took his notebook out of his pocket. "And you didn't like that idea?"

Higgs shook his head. "There's nothing wrong with the lights we have. They're plenty bright and won't keep people awake."

Palmer started writing in his notebook.

"Couldn't you just buy light blocking curtains?" I asked.

"Absolutely. But that's not the point. Most of the neighborhood didn't want them. He planned to push them through anyway. When it comes right down to it, he can spend the money however he wants and most people won't complain."

"What exactly did you say to him that had someone tell us we should talk to you?" Palmer asked.

"I said we'd keep the old lights, no matter what. I didn't care what I had to do, even if I had to take him out."

I frowned.

Higgs threw up his hands. "I was frustrated by the way he was railroading over what most of the neighborhood wanted. Again. He was a bully, and I was sick of backing down and letting him have his way."

"His wife said they were moving to Arizona soon. Why would he care what kind of lights were at his old house?" I asked.

"Like I said. He was a bully. The only thing that mattered to him was that he won every argument he was in."

"So after you threatened his life, what happened?" Palmer asked.

Higgs paled. "I didn't threaten his life. I was going to run against him in the next election. I was going to take him out of office."

I stood up and let him have my seat.

"I would never threaten to kill someone. If you were at the meeting, I think my context would have been clear." He paused for a moment. "Who told you about the meeting?"

Palmer shook his head. "We don't reveal our informants."

Higgs took a large gulp of coffee. "I bet it was Karen Jones."

Palmer said nothing.

Who was Karen Jones? She certainly wasn't our informant.

"Where were you early on Friday morning?"

"I was at home, asleep. I was so angry at Peter that after the meeting I went out for a drink. One led to two, then a few more. I didn't wake up until after noon that day."

"How did you get home?" Palmer asked.

Higgs shook his head. "Someone called me an Uber. I know because I've got the charge on my app, and I had to go get my car the next day."

"So you don't actually know what you did after a few drinks?" he asked.

Higgs flushed. "I know I didn't go and kill someone."

Palmer raised an eyebrow in disbelief.

"Check with Uber. They'll tell you where I was. There might even be a recording," he said.

"We'll be sure to do that."

Higgs stood up and put a hand to his mouth. "Oh no, wait here," he said as he rushed out of the kitchen. He didn't close the bathroom door tightly, and we could hear him retch.

Palmer took a look around the kitchen. "I think we're done here for now."

Outside the house, Elise Collins was waiting for us. "I hope you're arresting Marlon. I didn't want to say anything in front of Bess, but he's a blackout drunk and has no idea what he does most nights."

"I didn't know you knew them well," I said. She'd seemed unhappy Bess was with Mindy yesterday, and I had the definite impression they were not friends.

"I don't. But you should hear the things Bess says to excuse his behavior. It doesn't take long to figure out what's going on in that house," she said.

"We can't comment on an ongoing investigation."

Elise clenched her fists. "He's obviously the murderer. They argued earlier in the week. How much more proof do you need?"

"Thank you for your concern, ma'am, but I think your time is best spent taking care of your friend," Palmer said.

Her eyes flared open and then, without saying another word, she turned and stomped back into the Cafferty house.

"That was odd," I said.

"People get weird when they think they know who the murderer is. They demand we arrest their suspects no matter what. It's why we never comment on investigations."

The Cafferty's front door opened again, and Elise stormed out. I rolled my eyes, ready for her to start yelling at us again.

"And another thing, detective, if you were even half the man you ought to be, you'd be in there, protecting the women and children of the neighborhood. How do you think Mindy feels, living next door to the man who murdered her husband?"

Her voice had been growing steadily louder, and people were starting to look out their windows to see what the commotion was all about.

"Ma'am, I'm afraid I have to ask you to go back inside," Palmer said.

"No," Elise practically screamed.

Mindy ran out the door to join us. "Elise, please," she said in soothing tones. "I'm fine. I've got you, and I know the police will find Peter's . . . the person who did this, as soon as they can." She took Elise's hand in hers. "Please, come back inside."

Elise shook her hand free. "Not until they tell me they're going to arrest Peter's killer before the end of the day. I don't think I can take another night of worrying about what might be happening to you while I'm not around."

"Elise, please. You're making a scene. Come into the house, and I'll make you a cup of tea. We can both settle down."

"Listen to your friend, Mrs. Collins. Go inside and calm yourself down," Palmer suggested.

"I'd hate to have to call the chief and demand you do your job," Elise said just before she turned and walked into the house with Mindy.

I arched an eyebrow at Palmer. "Seriously?"

He frowned. "We hear that all the time. Usually it's an empty threat, but when it's not, he's got our backs. It's part of his job to deal with the public thinking they know more than we do."

That sounded horrible, but before I could say anything, Palmer's phone rang. He put it on speaker and said, "Hi Kate. You're on speaker with Isabella and me."

"Hey boss, we've found video that might give us Mr. Subramanian's alibi."

My heart started to beat faster. "You did? What is it?"

"Papatonis found a home security camera across the street that caught him leaving the house at four thirty and walking past every ten minutes or so for an hour."

"That's great, Kate. Get a copy of the video and we'll meet you back at the station. And then I want you to follow up on an Uber ride Marlon Higgs said he made the night Peter Cafferty was murdered."

"Will do," she replied.

He hung up and turned to me. "Unless you need to get back to work?"

I looked at my watch. "Yeah, I probably ought to check in on Mackenzie. I'm not used to feeling like I can take off and leave everything to her."

LISA BOUCHARD

Chapter 12

Palmer dropped me off at the apothecary, and we made plans to make plans to see each other outside of a homicide investigation. He was too busy to commit to a time and, with the holidays coming up, I wasn't sure I had much time to see him either.

I walked into the apothecary to see Mackenzie waiting on four different customers. We were never this busy—what was going on? I chose the oldest customer to wait on first. Mr. Oates was in his eighties and walked with a cane. I didn't want his bad leg to start hurting. "Good afternoon, Mr. Oates. How can I help you today?"

He smiled at me. "I'm not sure. I'd like to buy a Christmas gift for my lady friend, and I thought you could advise me."

"Absolutely. What did you have in mind?"

"Something romantic, but," he leaned in closer to me, "not too romantic. I don't want to give Florence the wrong idea about me."

"Florence? Do you mean Mrs. Dalton?"

"She's a lovely woman, my Florence. I only wish I'd met her sixty years ago."

I led him to the candle section of the shop. "I know she likes the lavender-scented candles. Do you want to get her one of those?"

He picked up the largest lavender candle I had. "I'll take this one."

"I'm sure she'll like it. Do you have plans to spend the holiday together?" I asked.

He sighed. "I wish we did, but she's spending the day at her granddaughter's house. The whole family is there, and it's one of the only times she sees everyone, so no. But we'll spend New Year's Eve together."

We walked to the cash register. "That sounds lovely. The candle is fifteen dollars."

"Before I pay you, do you have any tea that will help us stay up until midnight? I haven't been up past ten o'clock for years now."

Immediately I thought of the gunpowder green tea. "I know just the thing. It'll help you stay awake, but won't keep you from falling asleep when you want to."

"Sounds perfect," he said.

"It's the silver tin on the top row of the tea display," I said.

He took one box down and set it on the counter next to his candle.

I rang his order up and wished him a happy holiday. As he walked out of the shop, I looked around and Mackenzie was helping our last customer. I was pleased to see she could work through a group of customers so quickly.

The door chimes rang, and the entire Subramanian family walked in. My landlord entered first with his wife, Nila, and behind them were Prashad and his wife, Heather, walking arm in arm. They were all grinning and laughing.

"There she is, the woman I owe so much to," my landlord said.

I smiled, but felt uncomfortable. "It's nice to see they let you out so quickly, Prashad."

Prashad took my hand and shook it hard enough to hurt. "I'd still be in jail if it weren't for you, Miss Proctor. Thank you."

I pulled my hand out of his grasp and flexed my fingers. "You're welcome, but honestly, your lawyer was the one giving you good advice. He deserves most of the credit."

"Nonsense," Mrs. Subramanian said. "Manit told me how you intervened with your detective friend and kept our son out of prison, and even from being charged. Without you, he might still be in jail."

"I apologize for being a jerk to you the first time we spoke. I thought you were taking advantage of my father and promising him things you couldn't follow through on."

I shook my head. "I didn't promise him anything, other than I'd try to help you."

"Be that as it may, I didn't make it easy for you to continue to care about me. I'm sorry, and I'm truly grateful for everything you've done for me."

I got the feeling that if I continued to tell him I didn't do much, he'd keep thanking me, so I decided to end it there. "You're very welcome. I'm glad the police were able to confirm your alibi."

"Manit and I have been talking," Mrs. Subramanian said, "and we think it's only fair that we offer you free rent for a year."

I put my hands up as if to slow them down. "Oh, no. That's entirely unnecessary."

"If you saw the bill we got from the lawyer and then imagined what we'd have had to pay him to go to court, trust me, the family is saving money."

"I appreciate that, but I'm afraid it could look bad. Prashad is released and, right after that, the lead detective's girlfriend gets free rent. I wouldn't want that kind of trouble for him, or for you."

Mr. S. frowned. "We hadn't considered that."

"Please, don't worry about it. I'm happy I could help, and that's enough for me. I'm sure you have a lot to talk about as a family, and I don't want to keep you."

I hated to push them out of the shop, but it was starting to fill up with customers, and Mackenzie was getting swamped again.

They left and I helped customers for the rest of the day. By the time I hung the "closed" sign, I was exhausted. "I don't think I've ever seen that many customers here in one day."

"I haven't either, but I've noticed a definite rise in customers as we get closer to Christmas," Mackenzie said.

I surveyed the shop and saw inventory was way down on many shelves. "You head on home. I'll restock the shelves and get a head start on things I need to make, and I'll see you tomorrow."

She grabbed her coat from the office.

"And, Mackenzie," I said.

She turned back to look at me. "Yes?"

"I'm really glad I hired you."

She beamed at me. "I'm glad too. Thanks."

I didn't get out of the shop until eight that night. I put everything I could out on the shelves and made a list of everything I needed to make, in order of importance. As I sat at my desk, looking over everything I had to do, I realized I should probably get started. Problem was, I was exhausted.

Better to go home, get a good night's sleep, and start fresh in the morning. Making mistakes working tonight because I was tired wouldn't help anyone.

Not to mention making mistakes on magical items could have serious consequences.

I put my coat on and headed for home. It was crisp and cold out, so I walked fast. Halfway home, Jameson joined me on the walk.

"Hey, I've got a question for you. You know the sorority doesn't have enough familiars, right? How can we get more?"

Jameson stopped walking. "The first thing to do is get my family away from the fraternity."

"Of course we will. I promise. I just don't think the sorority is ready to help yet. We can't seem to agree on anything."

"I'll talk to Hope's familiar. Until then, we've got a lot of work to do tonight."

My heart leapt. "Are we finally going to learn teleportation?"

He didn't answer, so I continued.

"If not, I'm too tired. I just want to have dinner and go to sleep. We're almost sold out of half the shop, and I need to spend tomorrow making more products for the apothecary."

"You're not ready for teleportation, not on your own at least. It takes years for a witch to learn how to move from place to place safely, and you need to start practicing with small objects."

I rolled my eyes. "How long did it take you?"

"Three months," he said. "But it's easier for familiars."

I opened the door to the apartment building. "Of course it is." I didn't talk to him in the hallway, because even though lots of people talk to their cats, most don't wait for an answer.

I tiptoed past Bruce's apartment and didn't breathe until I'd closed my door behind me. Maybe he was out, because it was rare that he didn't at least open his door to see who was walking by.

Jameson levitated a can of cat food from the cabinet and used more magic to open it for himself. "It's about time to start teaching you the basics of teleportation. Eat dinner and we'll start tonight."

I grinned. I'd wanted to learn this skill since I'd seen it used in my shop by one of the fraternity. "Excellent." I pulled out a ready-made meal from my freezer that Palmer had dropped off weeks ago. I wasn't sure what was in it, but I didn't care. It was going to be delicious. How had I gotten so lucky to find a man who cooked for me and let me interrogate his suspects?

Once I pulled the container out of the microwave, I saw dinner was meatloaf, mashed potatoes with gravy, and green beans. I should have eaten it slowly and enjoyed it, but I couldn't wait to start working with Jameson on my new skill.

"Sit on the couch and put a coin on the coffee table," he said.

I pulled a penny out of my pocket and put it on my new coffee table. "Now what?"

"Focus on where the penny is now, and where you want it to be." He jumped up on the couch and sat next to me. "You want the penny to move just an inch. Anything further could be a disaster."

I thought he was being a little overdramatic, but I'd learned to listen to him and let him guide me.

"Is this something the amulet can help me with?" I asked, pulling it out from under my sweater.

"It will, but I want you to start without it. The stronger you are without the amulet, the better you'll be."

I released the amulet. I had to be holding it to channel its help into my magic, and just wearing it wasn't enough. At least not yet. I focused on the penny, and a spot an inch away on the table.

"This next part is tricky," he said. "You need to focus on the penny appearing where you want it to. Not moving through space like it would if you pushed it from one place to another, but appearing in the new location as soon as it disappears from the old location."

My high school physics teacher would have something to say about this—momentum, quantum tunneling, energy and mass relationships—he'd definitely think the penny couldn't move.

I put him out of my mind and focused harder. With my eyes closed, I pushed my mind to the limit. I felt the penny move and heard a screeching sound in front of me.

My eyes flew open. "What was that noise?" My jaw dropped open as I saw the penny embedded into the surface of my new table, eight inches away from where it started. "Oh, bats!" I whispered.

I reached out and tried to pick the penny out of the table, but it was stuck.

"It's not going anywhere," Jameson said.

"You didn't tell me I was going to ruin my new table," I said as I kept trying to pry the penny loose. "My eyes were closed. Did I do it or did I just push it?"

Jameson rubbed his face with a paw. "You did it. And now you know why it takes so long to master the skill. A penny is small and you drove it into the table. Imagine what would happen if you tried to move yourself halfway across town."

More mass, more energy, more room for disaster. I gulped. "I'd drive myself into the ground?"

"Possibly. Or you might appear in the middle of a solid object. There aren't any safeguards here, not even with the amulet."

Stifling a yawn, I reached out and scratched between his ears. "I see what you mean about needing practice. I'll definitely put more time into this."

He put his paw on my leg, a sign that he needed me to pay attention to what he was saying. "Only when I'm with you. You're not ready to practice alone yet."

The yawn won. "Excuse me. I was tired when we got here, but now I can barely keep my eyes open."

"You're working magic at the limits of your abilities. Of course you're exhausted. Sleep now, and we'll practice more tomorrow night."

SIMPLY IRISISTIBLE

Chapter 13

Two days later, Palmer pulled his car up next to me as I was walking to work. "Get in. There's been another murder."

My heart sank as I opened the car door. "Who?"

Palmer's lips were pressed into a thin line. "Marlon Higgs."

I hadn't expected that. "Cafferty's next-door neighbor?"

He nodded.

"Maybe Cafferty's murder wasn't about work, but about his neighborhood."

"I'm beginning to think that's true. Kate confirmed his Uber ride, so we know he didn't kill Cafferty. She and Papatonis have secured the scene, and she says there's a note from the killer."

I shuddered. What kind of person could be so callous as to write out a note after having taken a life?

I buckled my seatbelt as he sped off. "Mackenzie's opening the shop, so I've got all the time we need."

"Good. I'd like Thea to take a look at the note too."

"Do you think that'll work? It didn't with the statue."

We turned left onto the road the Caffertys and Higgses lived on. "I don't know. But if she's free, it can't hurt to give her a shot. There's something happening in this neighborhood, and we need to figure it out before anyone else is murdered."

We pulled up behind an unmarked cruiser. There were no neighbors gawking or even looking out their windows at the house, so word must not have gotten out yet.

"He was found behind the garage," Palmer said.

We walked around the garage and he held the crime scene tape up for me. "Morning, Kate, Papatonis," I said.

They were standing guard over Marlon Higgs's sheet-covered body, waiting for us. Kate pulled her notebook out and began to read. "Mrs. Higgs found her husband this morning as she was taking the trash out. They have separate rooms, and she doesn't know when he came home last night, except to say it was after eleven when she went to sleep."

Palmer nodded to Papatonis, who lifted the sheet up. Mr. Higgs had been hit on the temple and fallen, face down, onto the lawn.

"That the murder weapon?" Palmer asked, gesturing to a golf club by the victim's leg.

Kate nodded. "It's got blood on it, so we think so. The note was pinned underneath it. We've got photos."

Papatonis handed Palmer a plastic bag with an unfolded note in it.

Say NO to the HOA

"Is this really something to kill over?" I asked.

Palmer shook his head. "I wouldn't have thought so, until today."

Papatonis replaced the sheet over Mr. Higgs. "The wife's inside, with her neighbor."

"Not Mrs. Cafferty," I said.

Kate looked in her notebook. "Yes. She lives next door."

"And her husband was murdered earlier this week," Palmer said. "Wait here for the crime scene techs. We'll go talk to the wife."

I followed Palmer to the back door, where he knocked. Mindy looked over from the stove and motioned for us to come in. "Detective Palmer, I'm glad you're here." She took the kettle off the stove and began to pour hot water into three mugs. "Can I make you tea as well?" she asked.

Palmer said no and I followed his lead, even though tea would have warmed me up from standing outside over a dead body.

"Bess is in the living room. Come on in."

We followed her to the living room and saw the third person in the room was Elise. Mindy sat next to Bess and handed her a mug.

"I guess I'll go get mine in the kitchen," Elise said.

Bess looked to Palmer and me and said, "Please, sit down," before beginning to cry.

Mindy put her arm around her neighbor. "That's right, just let it all out," she murmured.

"Mrs. Cafferty, do you think you can answer some questions for us? We'll let Mrs. Higgs pull herself together before we talk to her," Palmer said.

"Oh, of course. But call me Mindy. Heaven knows we've seen enough of each other over the past week for that."

Palmer gave her a short nod, but did not invite her to call him Steven. "We have new evidence that points to someone being unhappy with your homeowner's association. Does anyone come to mind?"

She took a sip of her tea. "Peter was on the association board for over a decade, and there's always going to be someone unhappy with the regulations. It doesn't matter that they have to read and sign them before they're allowed to purchase their house, they still find reasons to complain."

"When we last spoke, we focused on his work, but now I'd like to ask you about the neighborhood. Has anyone been particularly vocal lately? Anyone you or your husband felt threatened by?" Palmer asked.

"No one in particular," she said.

Bess reached for a tissue and blew her nose. "What about that guy who was complaining so much this summer? What was his name?"

Mindy thought for a moment. "Oh, right. What was his name? Kiniry? Right. Vince Kiniry."

"Is he the one who lives in the tiny, ugly house at the end of the street?" Bess asked.

Mindy nodded. "Grandfathered in, or else he'd never be allowed to stay."

Palmer wrote the name down in his notebook. "Do you remember what he was upset about?"

Elise returned from the kitchen. "Mindy, I think we should go, give Bess time to grieve on her own."

I looked up at Elise. To the best of my knowledge, she hadn't left Mindy alone for days.

Mindy looked to Bess, who was barely keeping herself from crying. "No, I don't think so. Bess was here for me, so I'm going to stay. You've spent so much time with me, I'm sure you'd like to get back to your own house. I'll give you a call in a few days, once things settle down here."

Elise's lips thinned. She shot a hateful glance at Bess, turned around and left the room. A moment later, I heard her mug banging in the sink and the back door slamming.

Mindy frowned. "She must be exhausted, the poor woman. She's been taking care of me for days without a break. It will be good for her to go home and sleep in her own bed. A good night's rest, and she'll be able to handle the fact that I'm still moving to Arizona."

"So that plan hasn't changed?" Palmer asked.

Mindy put her mug down. "Yes. Peter"—she paused for a moment to take a deep, calming breath—"Peter and I were planning to move after the new year. I'll still move but, of course, I'll wait until your investigation is over."

"What else can you tell me about Vince Kiniry?" Palmer asked.

Bess burst out into tears. "I'm sorry. I don't think I can do this right now. I need to call my daughter, make arrangements for . . ."

Mindy squeezed her friend's hand. "Call Bekah, then go rest. Everything else can wait."

Bess stood up, unsteady on her feet. "Let me help," Mindy said as she put an arm around Bess. "We'll get you upstairs and lying down."

The two women slowly walked out of the living room and upstairs. I looked at Palmer. "What's going on in this neighborhood?"

"I don't know, but we'll figure it out," he said.

There was a knock at the door. I jumped up to answer it and let Kate in.

She looked around before speaking. "Hey boss, I've got some news."

Palmer looked to the stairs. "Let's go outside to talk. We're done here for now."

We walked behind the Higgses' garage, where Marlon had, thankfully, been taken away. "I'm going to call Thea," I said.

Palmer nodded as he and Kate began to talk about the evidence.

"It's me," I said when Thea answered her phone. "Can you come do your evidence touching thing again?"

She groaned. "Another murder?"

"Yeah. He was the neighbor of the man who got bashed in the head. Are you busy right now?" I asked.

"No. I was just heading into the office. Text me the address and I'll be right there," she said.

I texted her the address and waited for her at the front of the house. I thought it would be better if she could examine the evidence before it got logged in at the police station—fewer questions that way.

I looked up and down the street. Kids had already gone off to school and their parents were at work. It was deceptively quiet. What was happening with the people here? I couldn't imagine wanting to harm any of my neighbors. Maybe that was because I knew them all, and had grown up with them.

They weren't strangers to me and, maybe in such a new housing development, that sense of community hadn't formed yet.

Thea pulled up but didn't get out of her car immediately. I opened the passenger door. "You okay?"

She turned to me, face drawn. "Yeah. It's just . . . it was tough feeling the emotions attached to the last piece of evidence."

I knew she had a hard time touching evidence, and I felt bad for asking her for help again. "If you don't feel up to it, you don't have to. I'll let Palmer know it's too much, and he can solve this case like he's solved all the others."

Thea opened her door. "No, I can't do that. If I can help, I will."

We both shut our car doors and I took her hand when she walked around the car. "I'll be with you."

She smiled at me. "Thanks. That helps."

I led her to the crime scene, which looked surprisingly normal now that the techs were gone. The only clues to the murder were the golf club and the note in evidence bags.

Palmer smiled at Thea. "Thanks for coming so quickly. I appreciate your help."

I looked from Palmer to Kate, then back to him.

"Right," he said, realizing he needed to distract Kate for a few minutes. "Kate, go into the house and check on Mrs. Cafferty and Mrs. Higgs. Make them some tea or coffee, whatever. See what they tell you when I'm not there."

Kate's face brightened. "Absolutely. If they're hiding anything, I'll find out."

"Kate," Palmer said, "be gentle, friendly. Let them approach you with information."

She nodded, knocked on the kitchen door, and let herself into the house.

Palmer picked up the bag with the note inside. "Just the edge, if you can."

Thea took her glove off and reached one finger inside the bag to touch the edge of the paper. I held her other hand, willing my strength to be with her.

She gasped and pulled her finger out of the bag. Her face went pale.

"Let's get you sitting down," Palmer said.

We walked her to her car, the only private place we could have a conversation, and all sat inside. Thea took a shuddering breath. "I think it's the same person. Only this time they weren't angry, they were annoyed."

"Could you tell who it was?" Palmer asked.

"No. I don't think I'm going to ever see the person, but I can feel their emotions and see a little of what they see," she said.

"That's fine. Could you tell why they were annoyed?" Palmer asked softly.

"They didn't want to have to bother killing someone else, but thought they had to. They were frustrated, but I couldn't tell why."

Thea turned in her seat to look at us. "I'm sorry. I really thought I'd be more help in your investigations."

"Hey, don't say that," Palmer said. "You've confirmed there's only one murderer, and that's a huge help. Knowing the two cases are connected will narrow down our suspect pool, and we'll make an arrest sooner because of it."

Thea gave him a small smile. "Thanks. I had dreams of touching something and knowing who the murderer was immediately. I guess that's never going to happen." She brushed a tear from her cheek.

And thank the goddess it wouldn't. "Maybe it's not such a bad thing though. It would be horribly upsetting to see criminals every time you touched things. Not to mention, can you imagine how hard it would be to run your business? Who knows who's touched the money before it gets to you."

She shook her head. "I can see what the last person to touch an object felt, and a little of what was around them, so at least there's that. People hiring a tour company aren't usually murderers, so I think I'm safe."

Palmer put a hand on her shoulder. "You've made valuable contributions to this investigation. No one person solves a case, it's a team effort. So thanks for being part of the team."

My heart warmed. Did I have the best boyfriend or what?

"Are you okay to drive, or do you want me to get someone to bring you to work?" Palmer asked.

Thea held her hand out and it was shaking. "A ride would be good," she said.

"Wait here and I'll get Papatonis to bring you to work. Isabella can return your car later."

As Thea and Papatonis left in his cruiser, I thought about her and how difficult reading murder scene evidence must be for her. Thea wasn't inclined to complain about anything, so when she did, I knew it was very bad. "I don't think we should call Thea in unless we really need her."

Palmer blew out a long breath. "I was thinking the same thing. She's stoic, and for her to cry in front of both of us means it's taking too much of a toll on her."

"Thanks," I said, watching the cruiser turn at the end of the street.

"Want to go check on our next suspect?" he asked.

LISA BOUCHARD

Chapter 14

I remember!" I exclaimed. "I've been trying to figure out where I've heard his name before. Vince Kiniry is on the local cable station. He's one of the two people they have on air. He seems like a nice old man, I can't imagine he's killing people in his own neighborhood."

We drove through the neighborhood of large modern homes to the Kiniry house. I would have thought we'd left the neighborhood, because it was so much smaller and he clearly wasn't following the rules regarding landscaping, trash, or upkeep of his very small house. The only reason I knew we hadn't left the neighborhood was that his house was flanked by two that definitely belonged there. "This one?" I asked Palmer.

He doublechecked the mailbox. "Yup. I've seen this before, the property developer buys up all the good land surrounding a house in a good location, then tries to buy the one homeowner out. Kiniry must not have wanted to move at any price."

"So does that mean he's stuck following the rules even though he never signed up for them?"

"It's complicated. He doesn't need to follow the association rules as long as he doesn't use any of their benefits. The minute he starts using them, he's obligated to pay dues and"—Palmer made a face at Kiniry's yard—"follow the rules. Infractions this large, he's getting fined every week."

No wonder he was angry. The front door opened and Vince Kiniry stared at us.

Palmer unbuckled his seatbelt. "Let's go."

Kiniry opened the storm door as we walked up the front steps. "I have all the religion I want, I'm not buying anything and no, I'm not telling you who I voted for."

Palmer flashed his shield and Kiniry's smirk faded.

"This about the murder?" he asked.

"Murders," Palmer said.

"I guess you'd better come in then," Kiniry said.

We followed him into his house and took a seat at his small dining table. In contrast to the other homes in the neighborhood, his house had three small rooms on the first floor: a tiny kitchen, a living room that was split into dining area and tv watching area, and a small bathroom off the kitchen.

Kiniry wiped his face with his hand. "How many?"

"Two," Palmer said. "It looks like Marlon Higgs was beaten to death with a golf club."

"And now everyone in the neighborhood has decided I did it, haven't they?" Kiniry asked.

"Your name came up in our investigation. Right now we're checking alibis and eliminating suspects. Do you want to save everybody time and energy and just confess now?" Palmer asked.

Kiniry's head snapped up from where he had been staring at the table. "Absolutely not. It's no secret I'm unhappy here, but I'm hardly likely to be happier in prison, am I?"

Palmer's phone beeped and he looked at the text message before showing it to me.

TOD 4:30 am

"We can take you off our list if you've got an alibi for three to five this morning."

Kiniry's entire body relaxed. "I was at work with at least four other people from midnight to seven."

Unless the time of death radically changed, he was definitely not our guy.

"We'll look into your alibi. Will you be home for the rest of the day if we have questions?"

Kiniry nodded. "I'll be home, but I'll be asleep until five. You can come back then if you have anything else to ask me."

"I have one question, if you don't mind," I said. "If you hate it here and don't want to be here, why don't you just move?"

Kiniry furrowed his brow. "Is this part of your investigation?"

"Just answer the question," Palmer snapped.

"Fine. You don't need to get so huffy. I was here first, and I'm not letting someone, anyone, push me off my land. It may not be a fantastic house, but it was my parents', and they left it to me. I'm staying."

It was a position I could respect. If someone tried to push my family out of Proctor House, there'd be serious trouble.

"If I were to guess, I'd suspect the wives of it. Women are vicious, and we don't give them enough credit for that," Kiniry said.

We hadn't asked for his opinion, but now that we had it, I wondered. Had they killed their husbands? Had they pulled a *Strangers on a Train*–style victim swap?

"We're keeping an eye on both of them. Thank you for your time," Palmer said as he stood to leave.

Kiniry saw us out and once we were in the car, I asked, "You don't really think the wives did it, do you? I know you have to suspect the spouse, but even in this case? They seem so upset."

Palmer's stomach growled. "Want to grab lunch? We can talk about it then."

Lunch sounded fantastic. My coffee and pastry were still waiting for me at the apothecary, and I hadn't eaten anything all day.

~*~

Palmer had me call Kate as we drove through town and instruct her to check up on Kiniry's alibi. She said she'd get right on that, and we hung up.

"Where are we going for lunch?" I asked.

"My place. I've got leftovers, and we don't spend enough time together. I don't want to share what little time I have with you with anyone else today."

My heart may have fluttered a little. "Sounds great."

I hadn't been to his house since the showdown with Wolfe and the fraternity in his front yard. Truthfully, I'd been avoiding it. I'd stopped having nightmares about Wolfe and that day, but every once in a while, I still got scared.

"Are you okay? We can go somewhere else if you want," Palmer said.

I realized I was biting my lip and stopped. "No, it's okay. It's just, I need to tell you everything about the sorority."

He looked at me from the corner of his eye. "There's more?"

"You remember the guy named Wolfe, who was in my shop? He was trying to do some bad stuff in town. We had a showdown, I guess you could call it, with him in your yard."

He didn't say anything for a moment. "When you say we, do you mean your family?"

"Yes. And Jameson. It was a little touch and go, but we won and he disappeared."

He pulled the car into a convenience store parking lot and parked. "Are you in any danger?"

I shook my head.

He turned to look at me. "Am I in any danger?"

"No. He's gone, and I don't think he'll be back. And even if he does come back, he's after me and my family, not you."

"That doesn't make it better," he said through clenched teeth. "I'm a cop, Isabella. I protect people in danger. I can't believe you never told me this."

He gripped the steering wheel and didn't say anything else for a minute.

"I'm sorry I didn't tell you, but what could I have said? I don't think there was any way I could have explained it without telling you about magic."

He rubbed his face with his hand. "No, I don't think there was. You're not keeping any other secrets from me, are you?"

My heart stopped. I hadn't told him everything about the sorority, the fraternity, or the low-level struggle they were in. Now that he knew magic and the sorority existed, was there any reason to keep this from him? I wasn't sure there was. "Well . . . there's one other thing I haven't told you. It's not that it's a secret, but I wanted you to get used to the idea of magic before I sprang anything else on you."

His eyes narrowed. "Tell me everything."

My stomach growled. "I will, but why don't I tell you over lunch? It could take a while."

We drove in silence to his house. When we got to his front door, I didn't go in.

"You okay?" he asked.

I put my hand on his doorframe and said, "Yes. I'm putting a protective ward on your house, just in case. I can't believe it didn't occur to me to do this before."

When I was done, we walked into the house. "What does that ward do?"

I surveyed the inside of his house. The first floor was open concept with the living room in front, a dining room table behind the comfortable leather couch and then the kitchen at the back. For a single guy, he'd decorated it nicely in a black, silver, and white color scheme. "Wow."

He smiled. "You like it?"

"I do. I expected something more . . . bachelor-looking than this."

He took his coat off and hung it in the closet, then hung mine up as well. "You mean a horrible mess?"

I grimaced at the stereotype I'd had in my mind. "Sorry. Yeah."

We walked to the kitchen and he started pulling containers out of the refrigerator.

I started opening the plastic containers he handed me. "This is a simple ward that keeps people who want to harm you from entering. It works, unless you leave the door open or invite them in. I can come back a few more times to layer more wards on your house so that even if the door is open, people can't come in if they want to hurt you."

"So they just can't come in? Like a vampire?" he asked.

I chuckled. "Similar, except instead of feeling like there's a force keeping them out, they will suddenly have a very strong urge to go somewhere else. People wouldn't question that impulse as much as if they felt they physically couldn't enter your house."

Palmer took a frying pan out of a cabinet and set it on his stove. "That's clever." He sliced leftover roast beef thinly and set it on a plate. "Thank you for protecting my house. I appreciate that. So now can you tell me your big secret?"

I took a deep breath. "You know about the sorority, the seven witches in New Hampshire who are tasked with keeping magic secret from non-magical people."

He furrowed his brow. "Doesn't seem like you've done a good job, at least with me."

"You're a special case. There are other groups like mine throughout the world."

Palmer picked an onion out of a bowl and started slicing it. "It's the Sorority of Brigid, like in Saint Brigid? I didn't think witches believed in the saints."

I smiled at him. "We don't. Brigid was a Wiccan goddess long before she was ever a saint. Brigid protects and watches over wise women, and that's why we're named for her."

Palmer put olive oil in the frying pan and turned the burner on. "Okay, that's not a bad secret. But you wouldn't have formed this group if there was no one to fight against. Let me guess, Wolfe?"

I blinked back the tears from the sliced onion. "The sorority started to keep witches safe from everyone else. Over the years the focus has shifted to men like Wolfe. He's a member of the Fraternity of Free Witches. They want everyone to know witches exist. Their plan is to take over the world, having witches in charge and non-magical people as their servants."

Palmer set his knife down. "You're kidding me, right?"

"Not even a little. I'm new to the sorority, and all I can say is the fraternity hasn't succeeded here."

Palmer scraped the onions into the heated pan and seasoned them with salt and cracked pepper. "Is your whole family in the sorority?"

"Definitely not. Grandma has always been against anyone in the family joining the sorority. I didn't even know it existed until I inherited my amulet from Mrs. Thompson."

He turned from the stove to look at me, mouth open. "Beatrice Thompson? Your neighbor?"

"Yes. I inherited my amulet and Jameson from her." I fished out my amulet from under my sweater and showed it to him, even though I was sure he'd seen it before.

Palmer shook his head and turned back to the stove. "So how many people are in the fraternity? Do they have limited numbers too?"

The smell of the cooking onions made my mouth water. "I have no idea. I can tell you the names of a few, including Wolfe and Forster."

"Forster? Why am I not surprised? This puts him on a whole new level."

I took a glass from the drying rack next to the sink and poured myself some water. "Yeah, he's bad news no matter how you look at him."

Palmer put the sliced roast on the bed of onions and turned back to me. "So what you're saying is there's an entire shadow war being fought that non-magical people know nothing about."

I frowned. "I don't think 'war' is the right word. At this point, it feels like the fraternity is checking the borders, probing for weaknesses, seeing what they can get away with before any serious assaults."

"Wouldn't hunting down the older witches count as a serious assault?" he asked.

I took a sip of water. "Yes. Taking out our strongest witches, whether they were in the sorority or not, has weakened the law-abiding magical community that stands against the fraternity."

He pulled a can of soda from the fridge and sat at the kitchen island. "It's a lot to take in."

"I know. I never wanted to keep anything from you. I just wanted to make sure you were ready to hear what I had to say."

He took a long drink of his soda and set the can down. "How can I help? Or how can the department help?"

"Well, first thing is you can't tell anyone what I've told you. Even the chief doesn't know about the sorority." I thought for a minute. "Honestly, I'm not sure there's anything you can do that you're not already doing. Just be prepared for an emergency call where I need, where we need your help."

He reached out and took my hand in his. "I'm not sure that's enough. What else can I do?"

I frowned. I didn't want to tell him he was trying to fight above his weight class, not when he was trying to protect me. "Nothing. I'll let you know when it's time for more."

SIMPLY IRISISTIBLE

Chapter 15

I left the apothecary promptly at six, because Hope had planned a training event for the sorority. I'd hoped to grab dinner, but the minute I walked into the kitchen of Proctor House, Grandma shooed me into the living room. "They're all waiting for you."

I wasn't sure why Proctor House had to be the sorority's training ground, but it was better than having to travel an hour or more, so I didn't complain. When I walked into the living room, six pairs of eyes looked to me.

"Oh, good. Isabella, you're here," Hope said.

I took my coat off and tossed it across the back of the couch. I squeezed into the one remaining seat between Anna and Claire. "Now that I'm here, what are we doing tonight?"

Hope stood and started to walk across the room. "We are beginning to practice working together. Just because the fraternity has seemed quiet doesn't mean they aren't planning anything, and we need to be prepared. The five older members have worked well together in the past, but Isabella and Helen have never worked with us. I'd like to do some simple drills in the backyard, testing how well we work together and looking for any places we can improve."

It was twenty-four degrees out and starting to snow. From the looks of the other witches in the room, no one wanted to work outside tonight.

"Outside? Why don't we stay here, where it's warm?" Helen asked.

Claire and Christina's eyes widened. Apparently we don't complain about what we're asked to do in this group.

"Hope is our leader, and we do what she says. I know you're new here, but we follow our leader, and this is why our sorority is so effective," Claire said.

I stood up and put my coat back on, hoping to lead by example. I might have been the youngest witch there, but at least I understood how to work in a group.

We walked through the house to the backyard, Helen still grumbling about needing to work outside.

"Isabella, if you would cloak your backyard for us," Hope said.

I cloaked the backyard and nodded to Hope.

"Very good, ladies. We're going to start with passing a spell between ourselves." A glowing ball of fire appeared in her hand and she tossed it to Sasha. Sasha lifted her hand and the fire stopped in front of her. She turned her hand and pushed the spell to Claire, who also stopped it.

Jameson had not taught me how to capture and then use another witch's spell. *Jameson, help! How do I catch and use another witch's spell?*

I heard his yawn in my mind. I must have woken him up. *Why do you need to do that? What's happening?*

Hope is insisting we practice together. I don't want to look like an idiot. How do I do this?

When the spell is sent to you, hold up your hand and imagine a large web closing over the spell. When you release the spell, let the web float away and then you push the spell out as though you were casting your own spell, toward another person.

That seemed easy enough, but rarely was magic easy the first time. I watched the glowing orb move from Claire to Anna and tried to focus on how she caught it. Anna passed it to Christina, although a bit shakily. Christina passed it easily to Helen, who then passed it to me, but with a faster speed none of the other witches had used. I barely got my hand up in time to slow it down enough for my imaginary web to catch it.

I turned to Hope and pushed the spell out, letting the web vanish. It may have gone a bit slower than everyone else's spells, but it got to Hope. When she caught the orb, she extinguished it. "Very good, ladies. Isabella, has anyone taught you how to do this yet?"

I shook my head. "Not exactly. Jameson just explained it to me while I was standing here. That was the first time I'd ever tried."

Christina scowled at me. Apparently she'd wanted to see me fail and didn't count on me asking for help telepathically.

"All right ladies, next I think we should—"

I interrupted Hope because I'd just had a great idea. I didn't think the other sorority members would ever start to respect me if I didn't show them how well I could protect people in real-world situations. "Instead of drills, I know a neighborhood that needs protection tonight. Maybe we could practice on a more real-world situation."

"That's an interesting idea. Tell me more," Hope said.

"I'm working with Detective Palmer on a case where two men, neighbors, have been killed just days apart. We could practice our skills there, keeping our eyes out and making sure there's not a third murder tonight."

"Absolutely not," Christina said.

Claire nodded. "There's no way I'm going to waste my talents keeping a bunch of non-witches safe. What they get up to in their own time doesn't concern the sorority. If they want to kill each other, fine. I don't care."

I was astonished. "I expect to hear that from the fraternity. Aren't we better than they are? Don't we stand for the idea that all life is valuable?" I knew they couldn't argue with me on that point.

"Lay out your plan, Isabella. What do you want us to do?" Hope asked.

"First, let's go back inside." I turned and walked inside, hoping they'd all follow me, and would be happy I'd gotten them out of the cold, if only temporarily.

I brought them to the kitchen because I really needed dinner. Maybe we would all need to eat if we were going to be in the cold for a few hours. To my delight, there was a platter of sandwiches waiting for us on the kitchen table. Soup was warming on the stove, and all the bowls, plates, and utensils we'd need were set out for us. I made a mental note to thank Aunt Nadia in the morning.

I took a plate and loaded it down with a half a ham sandwich and half an egg salad sandwich. Aunt Nadia didn't mess around when she made sandwiches, and I wasn't sure I'd even finish what I took. I set the plate down and lifted the lid off the soup pot. "Chicken noodle. I'll serve it, it will be faster that way."

Once everyone had their food, I sat and looked at the other witches in my kitchen. I was bound to them whether I liked it or not, and we needed to find a way to work together. All but Hope were staring at me with hard eyes, unhappy that I'd taken over our training night.

"I don't know everyone's talents yet, so I'll start with Hope. Hope, you should change into your squirrel form and make your way through the backyards in the neighborhood. Climb around, look through windows, make sure everything looks okay."

Hope smiled. "That sounds like fun. I don't get nearly the running around time I used to."

"I thought the rest of us could cloak ourselves and walk through the neighborhood. Unfortunately, with the snowfall, our footprints would be too obvious. Can anyone else take an animal form?"

No one answered. "Okay, no problem. Is anyone strong in levitation? I can, but it's not something I can do for a long period of time."

Christina scoffed. "It's not hard. I can levitate for hours on end."

I smiled and ignored her attitude. "Fantastic. I'd like you to cloak yourself and look into houses. Just make sure there's no one breaking in or hurting people."

Christina's eyes flicked to Hope, who gave her a small nod. Nice to know I had Hope's backing for my plan.

"Next, I'd like to station one person at each of the remaining two association officers' houses." I looked at the women around the table and chose two at random. "Anna and Sasha, I'd like you to do that. I'll get you the addresses before we get there."

Anna and Sasha looked at each other and rolled their eyes. They said nothing, so I ignored their attitude and moved on.

"Before you give me some boring job, I can probe people for their intentions from a fair distance away," Helen volunteered.

I smiled at her. Was it possible someone was cooperating with my plan? "Excellent. You can stand by the entrance to the neighborhood and do that."

That left me with no job for Claire. I probably should have thought this out before I opened my big mouth. "Claire, you can..."

In a moment of panic, my mind came up with something. "You can drive through the neighborhood, changing the appearance of the car with each pass. The speed limit is slow enough, you'll be able to look around and see what's happening."

I sat back in my chair and took another bite of my sandwich. "Now we've got people moving both slowly and quickly through the area—we're bound to see if anything bad happens."

"What about you?" Claire asked. "You don't have a job yet."

Bats!

Hope answered before I could come up with something for myself to do. "Isabella will be the central point of communication for all of us. If we see anything, we let her know telepathically, and she'll relay the information to the rest of us."

I looked at my watch. "It's seven thirty. Let's finish eating and plan to get to the location by eight."

While the rest of the sorority was eating, I called Palmer. "Do you have anyone watching the Cafferty and Higgs neighborhood tonight?"

"And good evening to you too. I'm fine, thanks."

I walked out of the kitchen. "Sorry. We, the sorority that is, are going to use the area for a training exercise tonight, and I'm nervous because I'm in charge."

"I thought you were the youngest witch in the group, how'd you get put in charge?" he asked.

"It was my idea."

Palmer chuckled. "That's what you get for having ideas. No, we don't have anyone there tonight. When you say 'training exercise,' what exactly do you mean?"

"First of all, we're all going to be cloaked or disguised in some way, so you don't need to worry about complaints. We're just going to be watching what happens and making sure no one gets murdered," I said, hoping to keep him from worrying, or worse, checking up on us.

"No illegally entering houses, right?"

"Of course not."

"And calling me the instant anything happens?"

"Absolutely. My team would fade into the background as though we were never there."

"It's cold out tonight," he said.

I scoffed. "Do you think we can't keep ourselves warm? We'll be fine."

"Are you doing this because you think the murders are related to the fraternity?"

There hadn't been an inkling of magic near either murder scene. "No. Honestly, we just need to practice working together as a group, particularly since there are two new members."

"All right. Make sure you're all invisible, though. I don't want to answer a call about people loitering."

I laughed. "No one will know we're there, I promise. And can you text me the addresses of the last two officers of the association? I'm putting one person at each house."

"That's not a bad idea. I'll have to look them up, so give me a few minutes."

"I will. Thanks."

We hung up and I walked back into the kitchen.

"Chatting with your boyfriend?" Christina teased.

I blushed. "Yes. Because he's getting me the addresses we need." I really needed to stop blushing so much. What did it matter if I'd called Palmer? Even if I just wanted to talk to him, it was no big deal.

Two addresses popped up on my phone. "Okay, it's time to go." I sent each witch a telepathic picture of the neighborhood we'd be protecting tonight. "Remember, we're not there to be noticed, just to keep people safe."

As we walked outside, I asked Anna for a ride. "I suppose so. You'll have to sit in the back, though."

I looked into her car and her familiar was sitting in the front seat.

I climbed into the back seat and had to push a large bag of dog food out of the way.

"Why did you come up with this plan? We could have done an hour of practice and all gone home, warm and dry," Anna asked as we started driving.

This explained a little of their hostility toward me. "I thought it would be more fun to do something useful rather than stand around and do the witch equivalent of basic passing drills."

She looked at me in her rearview mirror. "You weren't doing so well with the simple things, and now suddenly you're in charge of our training, and dragging it out for the whole night."

"I thought Hope would be in charge, not me. And it never occurred to me we'd be out all night. I've got to work in the morning. I'm not retired like the rest of you, so this is worse for me."

She didn't say anything else as we drove, and I didn't feel the need to be more friendly.

Anna parked her car a block away and we walked to the entrance of the neighborhood.

Is everyone here? I asked.

Each witch checked in, saying they were.

Great. Keep your eyes open and let me know if you see anything.

I decided to do one walk down the street the Higgses and Caffertys lived on. It was dark enough already that one pedestrian wouldn't even be noticed. I took my time and looked at each of the houses. It was possible that someone here was a murderer.

I shuddered and walked a bit faster. I was tempted to check in on Mindy Cafferty, but I'd promised Palmer no one would notice us.

Ten minutes into our evening, I checked in with each witch individually. No one reported anything suspicious. At the end of the street, I stepped into the shadow of a pine tree and cloaked myself. I walked back down the street, enjoying the twinkling Christmas lights and trees in large picture windows. The neighborhood seemed so quiet and peaceful, but it wasn't. The murders had been reported, and I was certain the families in the area were worried and taking extra care to be vigilant.

Anna was the first to contact me. *Can I change assignments? There's a kid practicing violin in the garage at my house and I can't take it. My ears are about to start bleeding.*

Are you in the garage with him? I asked with panic.

No. But I have sensitive hearing. Can I trade with Sasha?

I rolled my eyes. How long would a kid practice an instrument? Half an hour? An hour? *Try to put up with it a little longer. He won't be there all night.*

Sasha was the next to complain. *There's no one at my house. This is a waste of my time.*

Sasha, go trade with Anna. There are people at her house. I found myself hoping the junior violinist would practice longer, just to teach Sasha not to complain.

A half hour later, Helen complained. *The wind is picking up and I don't have anywhere to stand to get warm. I'm checking the intentions of everyone who goes past me, but honestly, none of them have good intentions. I'm in the sorority to protect witches, and there aren't any here. When can we go home?*

This was getting out of hand. Hope? I'm about to have a full mutiny here. People are complaining and don't want to stay. What should I do?

Before she could answer, Claire contacted everyone. Hey Isabella, my car's about out of gas. I'm going to head out now. There's nothing going on here.

Wait, I said to everyone. We're not working together at all. Our plan was to protect these people tonight–

Claire drove past me and out of the neighborhood. I blew out a breath. "And that's what I'm going to do."

A squirrel started to walk toward me and, as it got closer, it changed into Hope. "We're the only two left."

I shook my head. "Broomsticks! I thought this would be better training in working together. I'm sorry I ruined it."

She put an arm around me. "It's not your fault. If I hadn't thought it was a good idea, I wouldn't have allowed it. We'll give everyone a few days to cool off and try something else."

I grimaced at the thought of trying this again. "You might as well go home. There's no team to work with anymore."

"I'll drop you off," she said.

"No thanks, I'm going to stay here and watch the neighborhood."

She looked at me, brows furrowed. "Are you sure?"

I nodded. "I'm not the kind of witch that leaves people in danger."

SIMPLY IRISISTIBLE

Chapter 16

I dragged myself into the Fancy Tart at eight thirty the next morning. Our training exercise hadn't lasted long, but I decided to stay and keep an eye on things for a few more hours. Nothing happened, and as the Christmas lights were turned off and people went to bed, I began to feel alone and vulnerable.

At two in the morning, I finally decided to go home. As I trudged down the snowy streets, a police cruiser flashed its lights and pulled up next to me.

"Isabella, is that you?" Kate's voice called out.

I bent down and looked inside the car. "Fancy meeting you here."

"Get in. Palmer would have my hide if he knew I saw you out here and didn't pick you up," she said.

I climbed into the car, grateful for the heat. "Thanks, Kate. Can you drop me off at home?"

She grinned at me. "It'll cost you."

I couldn't imagine what she wanted. "Extortion? From an officer of the law?"

She turned her lights off and started driving. "I'm desperate. I want to get the boss something for Christmas, but I don't know what."

I leaned back into the comfortable seat. "You and me, both. I've got no idea what to get him—I'm supposed to be shopping with Hannah McGinty on Friday so she can help me figure it out."

She turned left onto my road. "Should I even ask why you were out so late?"

I sighed. "I had this feeling, you know, something bad might happen tonight."

She pulled into my parking lot and stopped the car. "You thought something bad was going to happen and didn't call me? I thought we were friends."

I looked at her, astonished. "Of course we're friends. But I didn't call you because I was just checking it out. If anything had happened, I'd have definitely called you, or Palmer."

She frowned. "Not sure I believe that."

"I would have. I've got more respect for how much trouble I can get into on my own," I said.

She shook her head. "Palmer told me you can take care of yourself and that I shouldn't worry—Krav Maga, was it? But still, sometimes you need a gun at your side and you don't have one."

I hated that I couldn't tell her the truth, but there was no way I could explain the sorority to her. "I'm sorry. I didn't want to be a problem for you. If it makes you feel better, I called Palmer to tell him what I was up to."

Her eyebrows rose. "You did? And he let you come out here on your own?"

I yawned. "Excuse me. I think I should go inside and get some sleep. I'm at the apothecary all day tomorrow, and I don't want to fall asleep on my customers." I opened the door and got out. "Thanks for picking me up, Kate. I'll promise I'll call you if I need your help."

I closed the door and went into the building. It was eerily silent as I walked up the stairs. The security lights were the only ones on, casting long shadows in the hallway. At least I didn't have to worry about disturbing Bruce, my neighbor, at this hour.

I opened my apartment door to find Jameson waiting for me. "You're home late."

I rolled my eyes. "You wouldn't believe what happened. I'll tell you later though. I need to get some sleep."

Surprisingly, he didn't demand I explain everything to him. I was in bed within five minutes and sound asleep in six.

"Isabella? Can I help you?" Bethany's voice brought me out of my daydream.

I smiled at her. "Absolutely. One éclair and one cinnamon roll. It's going to be a long day."

Bethany looked me up and down. "You look like you've already had a long day."

I shook my head. "Nah. Just didn't get enough sleep last night. Can I get a double espresso too?"

She filled my order and met me at the register. "I thought hiring an assistant was going to free up your time, not keep you up at night. Is she working out?"

I handed her a ten-dollar bill. "Yeah, she's fine. Better than fine. I'd be lost without her. I was just up late last night—holiday rush, you know?"

She handed me my change. "Make sure you take a few days off after the new year, okay?"

A few days off sounded great. Maybe a few days away. Maybe a skiing vacation in the mountains. Who was I kidding? I didn't ski. But a "drinking cocoa and sitting in the lodge reading books" vacation sounded perfect. "I will. Thanks."

I unlocked the door to the apothecary and went through my morning routine. "Good morning, Trina," I said as I snapped my fingers and lit her memorial candle. "Have you seen how busy it is here these days? You'd be proud of how well the shop is doing. And I think you'd like Mackenzie too."

I turned to the shelf of tea to choose the flavor for the day. I'd drink a lot of it once I finished my espresso, so I chose my favorite, chocolate mint black tea.

Once I started the tea brewing, I looked around the shop. Mackenzie had restocked the glass jars on the herb wall, but the rest of our shelves needed to be filled. I walked into the prep room, taking my espresso with me.

Broomsticks! The new shelf I'd bought and filled with extra candles, tinctures, bubble bath, and other products was empty. I took a sip of my drink. Had we really almost sold out of so many things?

I opened the laptop in the office and checked the shop's bank balance. *Oh.My.Goddess*. There was one more zero at the end of the balance than I'd expected.

I drank the rest of my coffee as I let the idea of all that money sink in. When I finished, I opened the notes app on

LISA BOUCHARD

my phone, went back to the shop floor, and started typing how much I needed to make of which items. I was relieved I'd gotten ahead of my customers' special orders and wouldn't need to worry about them until after the holidays.

I looked at my completed list and sighed. This was more than I could do in a day and would probably use the rest of the ingredients I had in the prep room. I needed to prioritize and get to work fast.

Once I'd pulled down the ingredients for bubble bath, I heard a knock at the back door.

"Who is it?" I asked.

"Miss Proctor? It's me, Alex."

I unlocked the door to see Alex, the man I'd allowed to camp out at night behind the greenhouse. "Hi Alex, come on in."

He came in and followed me into the shop. "I've got tea—chocolate mint today. Let me pour you some."

People were much less likely to turn me down if I didn't ask if they wanted some. I poured the tea into a mug. "I suggest cream and sugar."

He nodded. "Sounds good."

I handed him the mug. "It's nice to see you. How's everything?"

He took a sip of the tea. "I'm worried."

I hadn't expected to hear that. "Let's go sit in the other room so I can work while we talk. I've got a lot to make, and we're in danger of running out of some products."

When we sat in the prep room, he continued. "Did you ask someone to check on the shop last night?"

I picked up the bottle of glycerin and poured it into a large mixing bowl. "No. Why do you ask?"

"Someone was out back late last night, checking the doors and windows."

"Were they trying to break in?" I asked.

He shook his head. "Not as far as I could tell. I didn't want them to see me, so I stayed in my tent. I'll move it closer to the edge of the greenhouse so I can identify anyone who comes tonight."

"I don't like that idea. Nothing in the shop is worth getting hurt over." I pulled my phone out of my pocket and dialed Palmer.

"Palmer," he answered. He must not have looked to see who was calling.

"It's me. Did you send anyone to check on the apothecary last night?"

"No. Why?" he asked.

"A friend of mine said he saw someone checking the door and windows out back. He didn't get a close look, though."

"I'm coming over to check it out. Lock your doors until I get there."

Sometimes I just didn't understand his reactions. He didn't worry when I was out all hours of the night trying to prevent another murder, but he worried about me in my safe little shop in bright daylight. "It's okay. They left when they couldn't get in, and my friend is here. We'll be fine."

Through the phone, I heard the chief call Palmer's name. "I've got to go, but I want you to call 9-1-1 if anything looks suspicious."

"I will, but honestly, everything is fine here."

I put my phone back in my pocket.

"Do you think the Peeping Tom is related to the case you're working on?" Alex asked.

I added five drops of lavender oil to the glycerin. "I doubt it. I don't ever mention the apothecary if I'm working on a case. I suppose someone could look me up online and find the shop though."

"What do you think about getting a motion sensing light for the back? Maybe with a camera as well? I could install it today for you."

I considered it for a moment. "I like the idea. But will the light wake you up every time an animal walks by?"

He finished his tea. "I'll set the sensor to register anything over three feet tall."

I added soap, honey, and water to the bowl and began to mix the ingredients together.

"I didn't realize you made the things in your shop. I assumed you bought them and put your labels on them."

"No. Trina, the previous owner, would never have stood for that." I put a funnel in one of the labeled bubble bath bottles and poured the honey lavender bubble bath into it. I filled the other six bottles, then set the bowl down. As I screwed the cap on each bottle, I infused the mixture with my intention.

"What was that?" Alex asked.

Had he recognized my magic? "What was what?"

"I don't know. You looked like you were saying a prayer or something over the bottles."

I smiled. "Oh, that. I add my wish that the person using the bubble bath receives the benefits from it. In this case, relaxation. Trina taught me to do that and, even though it's a little new-agey for me, it takes two seconds to do, and it's a way to honor her."

He stood up. "That's a lovely sentiment. I'm going to get to work on your new security light."

"Let me get you a bank card, hold on for just a minute." I walked into my office and found the spare business credit card. "Buy the light and camera and, if you need any tools other than a screwdriver or hammer, you should get those too."

He slowly took the card. "You're just giving me your credit card? What if I take off with it?"

I beamed at him. "I trust you. You're not the kind of man who would take advantage of me."

LISA BOUCHARD

Chapter 17

Alex installed my motion detector camera and light in the afternoon and returned my credit card. I knew he was an honest man and wouldn't steal from me. How I knew this, I couldn't say.

I left the apothecary at seven, exhausted from waiting on customers and trying to get as much created in the prep room as I could.

I didn't have the heart to go home and make myself dinner, so I walked to Proctor House. On the way there, I thought about how we could find the murderer. As I walked up the driveway, I had a stroke of inspiration.

I burst through the kitchen door of Proctor House and declared, "I have a plan!"

Aunt Lily looked up from washing the counter. "That's nice, dear. Any particular plan or just a general one?"

"It's a general idea, but I think Jameson and I can figure it out. Is he here?"

Aunt Lily looked toward the dining room. "Probably in there, lying by the fire."

I hung up my coat and bag and grabbed a biscuit from the table. "Jameson," I called out. "I need your help."

He meowed from the living room. I walked in to see him just as Aunt Lily said, lying by the fireplace. "I heard something about a plan?"

I sat on the couch and took a bite of my biscuit, crumbs falling to the floor. "What if the two widows were working together? They've got alibis for the time their husbands were murdered, but I don't think we ever checked to see if they had alibis for when their neighbor was murdered."

Jameson yawned. "I don't see how you need my help with this."

"I can't go back and question them on my own, but I thought you could teleport and take a look around their houses. If they were actually happy their husbands were dead, they wouldn't have to hide their feelings if they were alone."

He stood up. "I see your point. Might I suggest we check on our original suspect as well?"

I polished off my biscuit and wished I'd taken a second one. "Sure, why not? I doubt he did it, but a quick look around wouldn't hurt. Can you do it now?"

He jumped onto the coffee table. "No. This is a perfect training exercise for Jules and Jessamin."

I hadn't thought to involve them in an investigation. "But they're still young. I'd hate for them to get hurt."

"They'll be fine. They just mastered how to jump and cloak at the same time. They'll go together and, if there's a problem, I can jump to them and get them out in less than a second."

My eyes widened. That was much faster than it took me to move the penny on my coffee table.

"You'll be able to do it someday too. Have you been practicing?"

I hadn't been. "As soon as the holiday rush is over, I promise."

He jumped off the table and walked into the hallway. Jules and Jessamin ran up to him and stopped. It looked like they were all staring at each other, but he was most likely giving them instructions.

The three cats came back into the living room and sat on the coffee table. "Where does Prashad live?" Jameson asked me.

"Twenty-seven Thaxter Road. Do they know—"

The kittens disappeared. "I guess they do. How long will it take them to get back?"

"It shouldn't take long. They're going to go in, look around, and leave."

I watched the fire crackle and was about to get up to find myself some dinner when Jameson sat up, ramrod straight. "Something wrong?" I asked.

He closed his eyes and I didn't ask again, not wanting to break his focus. Jessamin popped back into the living room and then Jules, both barely on the edge of the table.

The kittens began meowing, and Jameson told them to settle down and speak one at a time. He turned to me and began to translate what Jules was saying. "They're upset you didn't tell them there was a dog in the house."

I reached out to pet Jules. "Oh bats, I'm sorry."

"The family was watching a movie together. There were no bags packed, nothing to indicate one or all of them were going on a trip. They were unable to search the entire house, because the dog somehow realized they were there."

I remembered that dog now. It could sense me when I was in the yard, but it couldn't quite pinpoint where I was. "Did they panic? Is that why they almost missed the table?"

"Yes. But for a first time, I'd say it was a solid effort."

The kittens continued meowing for a minute, then stopped.

"They're ready for a second assignment. One with no other animals."

I scratched Jessamin between the ears. "I'll poach you some salmon myself when we're done."

The kittens perked up at the thought of salmon.

"The next location is Bess Higgs's house. She lives at—" and the kittens were gone again. "How do they know where to go?"

Jameson rubbed at an ear with his paw. "They don't know where these houses are, but they can read your mind enough to see where they need to go. The magic does the rest."

Hold on a minute! "They read my mind? Can you read my mind? If you can, cut it out. Immediately."

Jameson looked at me, boredom across his face. "I could read your mind if I wanted to, but it's dull in there. You spend too much time thinking about customers and Detective Palmer and not enough time thinking about magic."

He was probably right. I'd also spent a fair amount of time thinking about what a pain in the cauldron he was. I hoped he hadn't noticed those thoughts.

He jumped in my lap and lay down. "Yes, I noticed those thoughts. They're normal, and you're a serious pain in my whiskers too."

I pet him and thought one more thought at him. *But we're a great team.*

Yes, we are.

Jules and Jessamin reappeared, this time in the middle of the table.

"Better trip this time?" I asked.

The three cats talked to each other and then Jameson looked up at me. "There were two women in the house, one older than the other. They were looking through photo albums and drinking wine. There was a suitcase in one of the bedrooms, but it was only half full and, given the difference in size of the two women, Jessamin thinks it belongs to the younger woman."

I pursed my lips. "That makes sense. Bess called her daughter once Marlon's body was found. I wouldn't worry about them."

Both kittens yawned so deeply that I could see all their teeth. Sharp, razor teeth that I never wanted to get in the way of. "Do they file their teeth, or are they born that way?" I asked.

"Born that way. They'll fall out, like human teeth do, and the new teeth won't be as sharp," Jameson said. "They're exhausted, though, and I don't think they can make another trip. I'll go to the other widow's house."

He didn't even ask where she lived before he disappeared. I looked at Jessamin and Jules, who were trying to stay awake, but were having a hard time keeping their eyes open. "I feel you, little dudes. Why don't I poach you some salmon? You worked hard tonight."

Jules let out a little purr and rested her head down on the coffee table, sound asleep. Jessamin flicked her tail and fell asleep next to her sister.

I had no idea how to poach salmon, so I pulled my phone out of my pocket and googled a recipe. I didn't think wine was good for cats, and I knew onion wasn't. I stood up, deciding I needed Aunt Nadia's help.

I found her in the kitchen, taking a paper-wrapped package out of the fridge. "I think the kittens need a snack," she said.

She was right. She was always right about what people needed from her kitchen. Just like I could tell what potion a person needed when I looked at them.

"They did some investigating for me and are asleep now. I don't think it helped that I forgot to warn them about a dog at one of the houses."

Aunt Nadia unwrapped the salmon and set it on the counter. She poured chicken stock into a small pan and warmed it on the stove.

"I was going to do this for them, but the recipe I looked up had wine and onions. I was pretty sure neither of those would be good for them."

She handed me a pair of oven mitts. "You're right. I'll take care of this. Why don't you take the plate out of the oven and have that for your dinner."

I took the plate out of the oven and removed the aluminum foil. I kissed her on the cheek and grabbed a fork from the silverware drawer. "You're the best," I said as I looked down at the eggplant parmesan she'd made me. "I'm going to wait for Jameson in the living room."

Honestly, I'd expected him to come back as quickly as the kittens had, but he wasn't waiting for me on the coffee table. I ate my dinner quietly, trying not to wake the kittens. He still wasn't back when I finished and brought my plate into the kitchen.

"Just in time," Aunt Nadia said. "You can bring these to the kittens."

I took the plates of salmon from her. "They're sound asleep, can the fish stay out until they wake up, or should we put it in the fridge?"

She laughed. "They'll wake up at the smell, eat, then go back to sleep. Just like all babies."

She was right. I'm not sure either fully opened their eyes, but they ate and fell asleep again. I was starting to get worried about Jameson. What was he up to? Was something bad happening at the Cafferty house?

I considered speaking with him telepathically, but I didn't want to disturb him. If he needed help he'd let me know.

I pulled out my phone and started looking at the list of ingredients I needed to order for the apothecary. The first three items needed to come from The Moonlight Altar in Connecticut. I pulled up their website and made the order. One less thing I'd have to do tomorrow. I was halfway through ordering the tinned teas I sold when Jameson returned.

"Are you okay?" I asked.

"Fine. I think I found our killer," he said.

My eyes widened in surprise. "Who?"

He sniffed the air. "Is there any more of that salmon?"

"I don't know, Aunt Nadia made it."

I followed him out of the living room and into the kitchen. Aunt Nadia had left another plate of salmon for him on the table. There was a plate with two cookies and a mug of hot cocoa waiting for me too. We sat and I couldn't wait for him to finish eating before I asked questions. "Who is it?"

"A woman named Elise."

Elise? That didn't make sense. "She's Mindy's best friend. They said they've been friends since kindergarten. Are you sure?"

"Yes. They were fighting when I got there. Elise screamed at Mindy that she couldn't ignore her problems and move to Arizona. She couldn't just pack up and leave after the funeral."

"There's no reason she couldn't. How does this prove Elise is the murderer?"

He finished his food and licked the plate. "Do you think you could learn how to cook like your aunt?"

I shook my head. "I tried. I'm much better with potions than food. What happened after the argument?"

"Elise stormed out of the house but, on the way out, she took a pair of mittens from the pocket of Mindy's coat. I followed her and jumped in her car before she slammed the door shut. I expected we'd go to her house, but we didn't. She drove around the block and walked back to the neighbor's house. She put the mittens behind the trash barrels and left them there. We walked back out, got in her car, and drove away."

"That was weird. Why would she do that?" I asked.

"As she started to drive home, she was talking to herself. She said there was no way Mindy could leave if she was in prison. Finally, Elise thought she could be sure she'd never lose Mindy."

My jaw dropped. "We've got to move those mittens before they're found at the crime scene."

Jameson purred. "I already did. Once I realized what she was doing, I teleported from her car, picked up the mittens, and put them in Mindy's coat pocket."

I scratched between his ears. "Smart."

"And I know exactly how we can catch her and bring her to Palmer. You need to call Hope."

LISA BOUCHARD

Chapter 18

It didn't take long for Hope to get to Proctor House. "You've got another plan?" she asked when I let her in.

I took her coat and hung it up. "I do. Well, actually, it's Jameson's idea. But I think it's a good one.

"Jameson did a little spying tonight, and we learned who the murderer is. Her name is Elise Collins, and she's the first widow's best friend. Jameson caught her trying to frame her friend so they could always be together."

Hope sat at the kitchen table and looked at Jameson. "You're sure?" she asked him.

"Absolutely," he confirmed.

Hope grasped her amulet. "And we can't have the police arrest her on the word of a cat. All right, then. Let me get everyone else here." When she was done, she let her amulet drop to her chest. "This is important, so tonight I want to give the orders. We'll have a better chance of having them followed."

I nodded. "That's fine with me. I just want to catch her before she kills anyone else."

Over the next ten minutes, the rest of the sorority members arrived at the house. I could tell we hadn't given them nearly enough time to get over their feelings from our last time together. Unfortunately, there wasn't anything we could do about that.

Hope clapped her hands to get their attention. "Thank you all for coming. Tonight we're going after a woman who has murdered two men, and we're going to catch her."

Claire sighed. "Again with the non-witch protection duties? I'm out of here."

"Leave your amulet on the table as you go," Hope said.

The muttering and whispered complaints in the room came to an abrupt stop. I had no idea a witch could leave the sorority, or be asked to leave.

"The same goes for anyone else. We will continue these easy exercises until you all prove to me you can work together. I'd never trust you with anything dangerous the way you are now," Hope said.

Claire didn't take her amulet off, but she shot me an ugly stare.

"Here's what we're going to do. Isabella and I are going to drive to the murderer's house and attempt to apprehend her. The five of you will surround the house, cloaked, and capture her if she flees."

I'd looked up her address while I waited for Hope to arrive. I slid the paper I wrote it on over to Hope.

"Six Merryfield Lane. I expect you all in place before we get there," Hope said.

The five witches vanished.

"I don't know if this is going to work," Hope confided in me as we got into her car. "I've never seen resentment so high of a new witch."

"Is it my age? Is it Jameson?" I rubbed my temples. "What can I do to change their minds about me?"

"You're very young to be in the sorority, true. But the real problem is they see your family as hoarding familiars when there are witches who need them. This rankles more because the rest of your family isn't even in the sorority."

I shook my head. "There's nothing I can do about that. Jameson is the only one who can speed up the kittens' training, and sorority members don't seem to be angry with him."

Hope's eyebrows shot up. "They wouldn't dare. He has a lot of sway with the kittens, and they don't want to ruin their chances of getting one."

I didn't understand. "This explains why Helen and Claire are angry, but why the rest of them?"

Hope frowned. "Don't worry about it. They'll come around soon enough. And if they don't, I'll start asking them to leave. They'll come around quickly after that."

I decided to change the topic. "How are you going to catch her?"

"I'm going to walk up to the front door and ask to see her. You'll be behind me, cloaked, just in case she gets past me."

"That's it?"

"I'll say she's won a quilt in our church raffle. That usually brings people to the door."

I looked around the car. "But . . . we don't have a quilt."

Hope laughed. "Not yet, but I'll conjure one once we get there. It's the same for all you young witches—you need to get confident using your powers for anything you think important. You're an adult, not a child. You don't need to ask permission to do what you think is best anymore."

I let that sink in. I didn't have to ask permission to do things I thought were right. I ran my business that way, so why didn't I run the rest of my life like that?

Hope pulled up to Elise's house. "This the place?"

I looked at the number on the mailbox and nodded.

"Good. Cloak yourself and I'll let you out of the car," she said.

I cloaked myself and she opened my door. She reached in and conjured a red and green Christmas quilt from thin air. She pulled the quilt out and held the door open until she saw my footprints in the snow.

I looked around but didn't see any witches. I could feel the pull of their amulets, though, and knew they were all in position around the house.

Hope walked to the door and I followed in her footsteps. She knocked on the door and a man opened it instantly. He must have seen her on the walkway.

"Hello. I'm looking for Elise Collins. Is she in this evening?" Hope asked.

He looked surprised that anyone was looking for Elise. "No, I'm sorry, she isn't. She's taking care of her best friend." He leaned toward Hope and said, "Her husband was one of the men murdered this week."

"Oh dear," Hope said, sounding like she was afraid a murderer was on the loose in town. "Elise, she's your wife?"

Mr. Collins nodded.

"She won a quilt in our church's Christmas raffle. I've been trying to get hold of her, but she doesn't seem to be answering her cell phone. Could I leave it with you?"

"She won a church raffle? That doesn't sound like her. What church are you from?"

"Saint Kendra in the Woods," Hope said with such conviction that I almost believed her.

"I'm not familiar with that one. I'll have to check it out," he said.

Hope handed him the now fully wrapped quilt. "We'd be happy to see you on any Sunday morning. You have a nice night, and tell your wife we appreciate her support."

"I will. Thank you," he said as he closed the door.

Once we got back into the car, I uncloaked myself and burst out laughing. "That was awesome! I can't believe he bought your story."

Hope didn't look impressed. "Where are we going to find her?"

"I'll have Jameson check."

Are you awake?

Of course I am. Did you catch her?

No, she's not at home. Can you check to see if she's at Mindy's house again? If she's not, I don't know where else to look.

I waited for a moment, wondering if he was going to answer me.

She's not there.

"Jameson says she's not with Mindy. Now what?" I asked.

169

Hope started her car and drove halfway around the block. She parked, and five witches appeared from the shadows. If I didn't know who they were, I'd have been frightened.

We got out of the car and met them on the sidewalk. "Now what?" Claire asked.

Hope blew out a long breath. "We don't know where she is."

"Oh, great. Now I suppose you want us to spend the night searching for her. I've got things of my own to do, you know," Sasha said.

"We all do," Christina said. "And so we've decided we're done with all this. Call us when witches are involved. Until then, we're done following the kid and helping her try to impress her boyfriend."

Ouch! That stung. I was out here in the freezing cold to protect my town. I loved that Palmer thought I was a good investigator and that I had always caught my suspect, but that wasn't what motivated me. I opened my mouth to speak, but Hope put her hand on my arm.

They're not going to listen to you. Let me handle this. Hope's voice said in my mind.

"Ladies!" Hope said loudly to get everyone's attention. "Go home. You're no use if all you're going to do is squabble and refuse to do as I say. Quite frankly, you're embarrassing yourselves with your behavior. I suggest you reevaluate why you're even here."

That seemed harsh to me, but I'd never run a group of strong-willed women. But I lived in one. What would Grandma do if we started acting like this?

She'd tell us we couldn't have dessert for a week, or something small that would seem big.

"As of now, you're all on probation. I'll be speaking with each of you this week, and you'll need to convince me why you should be allowed to stay in the sorority."

My lips pursed. That was much worse than not having dessert for a week.

"If you're not prepared to continue with your life of service to the magical and non-magical communities, I'll take your amulet," she continued.

One or two witches clutched at their amulets through their winter coats. "You can't do that," Christina said.

Hope narrowed her eyes. "We'll see about that. I suspect your amulets and your familiars are fed up with the way you've been acting lately. There are plenty of other witches in New Hampshire that would love to be in your position, and would do as they're told."

"So now you want us to follow your orders blindly? That's not what the sorority is about. We're supposed to work together to keep—" Claire said, stopping as she realized she was beginning to make Hope's point for her.

"Exactly. We work together, and questioning what we're doing is part of the process. Complaining that it's cold when you can cast a warming spell is, quite frankly, a load of rat's tails—and you know it. Not wanting to work with 'the kid' is the same. Now go home and think about your place in this group."

One by one, the witches vanished until only Hope and I were left. "Wow. That was harsh. If I'm the problem, maybe I should leave instead," I said.

"It needed to be said and, no, you shouldn't leave. Discipline has been lax, and it's my fault. I hope I don't have to start over with a new group of witches, but I will if this lot doesn't straighten up and fly right."

I blew out a deep breath.

"Get in the car. I'm bringing you home and you're going to get some sleep."

I wanted to argue, but she continued. "Elise isn't going to vanish off the face of the earth tonight. If she's trying to frame Mindy, that means she's not planning to kill anyone else. You can tackle the problem again in the morning."

She was probably right. "Okay. But I'm getting up early."

SIMPLY IRISISTIBLE

Chapter 19

I was drying my hair in the bathroom, getting ready for my day of Christmas shopping with Hannah, when there was a knock at my door. Who could possibly want to see me before the sun was up? I tightened my bathrobe and opened the door to see Kate standing there.

She frowned. "Oh. You didn't get my message."

"No . . . I was in the shower." I stood aside for her to come in. "What's up?"

"We got an anonymous tip that Mindy killed both her husband and her neighbor. Apparently, we missed some evidence that the caller could lead us to."

So Elise finally called about the evidence she planted. "We missed something? That doesn't sound right."

"I know, right? But we're going to check it out. Palmer wanted me to pick you up on my way there."

"Oh. Give me two minutes to get dressed." I ran into my bedroom and threw on jeans and a thick turtleneck sweater. Wool socks and my warmest winter boots on my feet, and I was ready to go.

Kate was standing by the door when I left the bedroom. "Ready?"

I nodded as I grabbed my bag and a hat. "Let's go."

"You haven't thought of anything I could get Palmer for Christmas, have you?" she asked as we drove to the crime scene.

I hadn't given it a thought, but I didn't want to tell her that. "He's a great cook, maybe a unique cookbook or something for his kitchen?"

Kate laughed. "Palmer? Cooking? I can't see it."

"It's true, and he's good at it too. That's the only thing I can come up with right now. I still don't know what I'm going to get him either."

No one had bothered to hide the police presence on the street today. Two cruisers were parked in front of the Higgs and Cafferty houses, and uniformed officers were searching both yards. "What are they looking for?" I asked.

"According to the tip, Mindy left a pair of mittens at the second crime scene," Kate said.

Palmer opened my door.

"Thanks for sending Kate for me," I said as I got out of the car. "What does Mindy say about all this? I find it hard to believe she's the murderer."

I wanted to tell Palmer everything I knew, but Kate was still there.

"We haven't asked her yet. All she knows is we're looking for new evidence. Evidence that isn't where the tip said it would be, so we've widened our search."

We walked behind the Higgses' garage. Two officers were going through the trash they'd dumped onto tarps laid out on the ground. Other officers were raking through the snow in the backyard.

"Papatonis," Palmer called. "Any luck?"

Papatonis stopped raking through the snow and shook his head.

"Can I speak to you for a minute?" I asked.

He raised an eyebrow, but led me out of hearing range of the other officers. "What's up? Do you know something?"

"It's Elise. Jameson caught her planting the evidence last night, and he unplanted it back in Mindy's house."

Palmer frowned. "And you're just now telling me this?"

"I didn't know when, or even if, you were going to get a call. I was going to tell you this morning, but you sent Kate for me. Here I am, telling you as early as I could."

He rubbed at his temple. "How am I going to arrest a woman on the word of a cat?"

I giggled. "You could call him a confidential informant?"

"There are rules for CIs. It's not exactly spelled out, but the expectation is that they're human." He turned to look back at the people searching for mittens that weren't there. "No, we'll let this play out for a few more minutes, then we'll question Mindy. Elise is there with her, and I can provoke her enough to implicate herself."

"Can I be there?" I asked.

"Yes. Mindy's going to need someone to stay with her while her entire life comes crashing down around her."

Finding out your best friend killed your husband would be devastating. "I'll stay with her until we can arrange for someone to take my place. We won't leave her alone."

"Did Jameson say why Elise killed Peter and Marlon?" Palmer asked.

"She didn't want Mindy to move to Arizona. When Mindy said she was going anyway, Elise's only option was to frame Mindy for the murders. She'd go to prison, and Elise could continue to be near her."

Palmer grimaced. "That's . . . not a healthy relationship."

I shook my head.

"Okay, let's get this finished." Palmer whistled to get everyone's attention. "Obviously, the tip was a lie. You can all go, except for Kate."

Kate jogged over to us. "What's up? Why are you giving up so quickly?"

"We can't waste the whole morning on a tip. We'll get more if we interrogate her instead," Palmer said.

Kate looked at him suspiciously. "If you say so, boss."

If only the sorority witches had the same attitude toward Hope.

We knocked on the Caffertys' front door and Elise let us in. "Did you find anything?" she asked.

"I need to speak with Mrs. Cafferty," Palmer said formally.

A quick grin flashed across Elise's face, but she hid it quickly. "Of course. She's in the kitchen. I was just telling her she can't run away to Arizona and ignore her problems here."

We followed Elise and when we entered the kitchen, Mindy stood up. "Have you found anything? Can you tell me who killed my husband?"

"Unfortunately, no. We didn't find anything. I've called a halt to the search."

Mindy sat heavily in her chair. A tear ran down her cheek as she closed her eyes.

"What do you mean you didn't find anything?" Elise asked.

"The tip said we'd find a pair of mittens behind the Higgses' house, but we didn't," Kate said.

Elise furrowed her brows. "Are you sure you looked hard enough? Why would someone call in a tip that wouldn't pan out?"

"I'm sure," Palmer said. "Mrs. Cafferty, we'd like to see your mittens, if you don't mind."

Mindy opened her eyes. "My mittens? Someone told you my mittens were where Marlon was killed?"

"Yes, ma'am," Kate said.

Mindy stood up. "That's ridiculous. They're in my coat pocket, where I always keep them."

We followed her to the front hallway where she pulled her mittens out of her coat pocket. "See? Right where they belong."

"No. That can't be," Elise said before she could stop herself.

Palmer looked to Elise. "What do you mean?"

Elise didn't answer immediately. "If you were out there looking, you must have had a reason. Right?"

Mindy stepped in front of Palmer. "Elise, what have you done?"

Kate stepped in front of the door, and Palmer moved to block the hallway. Elise was trapped.

"You don't understand, Mindy. You'd never be happy in Arizona, without me. I put your mittens by where Marlon died, so you'd be convicted and we could stay together."

"You did what?" Mindy asked again, slowly pronouncing each word.

Elise shifted from side to side. "It was all Peter's fault. He's the one who wanted you to move. I tried talking to him, but he laughed in my face. He's the one forcing you to leave me. But you were so brave, not complaining about the move. I'm your best friend, I couldn't let you suffer like that."

Mindy began to shake. "Say it. Tell me you killed Peter."

Elise moved to pull Mindy into a hug, but she backed away. "I had to. Don't you see? I didn't have any choice. I didn't want you to find out this way, with other people around. I wanted to tell you privately, so you could thank me."

"Thank you?" Mindy yelled. "Thank you for killing the man I loved? What's wrong with you?" She turned to the coat rack and pulled an umbrella off it.

"He was going to take you away from me. I couldn't allow that. And he was so easy to manipulate. All I had to do was send him photoshopped images of him with Gwen Vandermeer and tell him to meet me early in the morning," Elise said. "He refused to change your plans, so I killed him."

Palmer grabbed Mindy's arm before she could hit Elise. "Okay, Mrs. Cafferty. Let the police handle this."

Kate jumped into action and had Elise handcuffed before she could move. "Elise Collins, you're under arrest for the murder of Peter Cafferty."

She continued to read Elise her rights while Palmer gently took the umbrella out of Mindy's hands. "Isabella," he said.

I nodded and led Mindy to the kitchen. "Let me make you some tea," I said.

She nodded numbly and stared out the window.

The whistling of the teakettle brought Mindy's focus back to the kitchen. "Tea's in the cabinet next to the sink."

I looked through her supply and chose a decaffeinated valerian and passionflower. She'd need the herbs to help stay calm once the true horror hit her.

She took the mug from my hand and blew across the top of it. "Do you think Elise killed Marlon too?"

I was sure of it, based on Thea's emotional reading of the note. "It seems likely. I'm sure the police will find out soon."

I sat across the table from her and heard the front door close. "The police are gone now. They've taken Elise away, and you won't ever have to worry about her again."

She let out a small sob and took a sip of tea. "I can't believe this is happening to me. It hurts too much to be a nightmare, but I keep hoping anyway."

I reached my hand out to hers. "I'm sorry you're going through this. Is there someone you can call to stay with you for a while?"

She shook her head. "I'd call Elise. What a fool I was, thinking she was my friend."

I didn't know how to console her. Then again, I doubted there were any words that could take her pain away. I studied her and saw there were no potions that could, either. She had to go through her grief first.

But maybe she didn't have to go through it alone. "How about Bess? If there's anyone who knows how you're feeling, it's her. And I'm sure she'd like to know what was happening in her backyard."

Mindy nodded and handed me her phone. "You call her. I'll just cry when she answers."

"Of course. I found Bess's number in the contacts and dialed.

"Mindy? Are you okay?" Bess asked when she answered.

"Good morning, Mrs. Higgs. This is Isabella Proctor. I don't know if you remember me, but I'm next door with Mindy, and she asked me to call you and ask you over."

Bess sucked in a short breath. "Is everything okay?"

"Mindy is right next to me. Can you come right over?" I asked.

She hung up and through the window I saw her rushing across her yard. She walked in without knocking and went straight to Mindy.

"Did they find . . ." Bess started.

"It was Elise," she said in a whisper.

Bess looked at me. "Elise? Elise Collins?"

I nodded.

My phone buzzed. I looked at the text message from Kate. *Elise confessed to both murders.* "The police have just told me she's confessed to both murders."

Color drained from Bess's face, and I thought she was going to pass out. I jumped up from the table and led her to a chair. "Deep breaths. Put your head between your knees."

She did as she was told and straightened up when she felt better. "I let that woman into my home. Her family has eaten dinner with mine."

Mindy reached over to take Bess's hand. "I'm so sorry. It's all my fault."

"No, it's not," I interrupted. "I don't know you well, but you don't seem to be the kind of woman who would purposely invite a murderer into her home."

Mindy grimaced. "But I should have known."

I stood up to make Bess the same valerian and passionflower tea. "How? She hid her intentions well. None of us who talked to her had any idea what she was up to. If Detective Palmer didn't notice right away, you can't expect you would too."

"But—" Mindy started.

"Drink your tea," I said. "You're not to blame for any of this. Elise is."

"Isabella is right," Bess said. "We should focus our anger on Elise, where it belongs, not on ourselves."

Mindy drank some tea and Bess accepted the mug I handed her. "What am I going to do now?" Mindy asked.

"It sounds like you had a good plan already. Move to Arizona and live the life you and Peter wanted. There's nothing virtuous about staying in this house and reliving your pain every day. I say you should leave it behind and enjoy the desert," I said.

"My daughter has wanted to move closer to me for years now. She'd be happy to buy your house," Bess said.

"Ladies, I'm going to leave you now. If you need anything, please don't hesitate to call the police. I'm sure they'll be back to take further statements when you feel ready."

Bess and Mindy stood up and hugged me. "Thank you. And please thank Detective Palmer for finding who killed our husbands," Bess said.

I smiled and saw myself out as the two women started discussing the price of Mindy's house. It was good they had something positive to think about. More grief would hit them soon enough.

SIMPLY IRISISTIBLE

Chapter 20

I left the Cafferty house and realized I had no ride. I needed a car of my own. But for today, maybe Hannah would come pick me up here instead.

She pulled up ten minutes after I texted her. I was grateful I dressed warmly, because the winter winds were starting to pick up. I thought about Hope's advice last night. I was an adult and didn't need permission to do what I wanted. I didn't need permission to cast a warming spell over myself. This was going to take some getting used to, because I was raised to use magic as a last resort, never as a first action, no matter how much easier it was.

The aunts insisted on this magic-last strategy to keep us safe while we were busy dealing with everything else childhood and adolescence had to offer. Using a quick spell in the middle of a high school dance could ignite some serious problems for us.

"You ready?" Hannah asked as I climbed into her car.

I shook off the sadness of the closed investigation. "You bet. Thanks for picking me up here. I hope you've got some good ideas for me."

"I've got one or two. You don't live here, do you?" she asked as we drove off.

"No. We just wrapped up the double homicide that was in the news."

Hannah's eyes went wide. "You were working on that?"

"Yeah. We caught the murderer about an hour ago. I'm sure it'll all be in the news by tonight. If you don't mind, I don't really want to talk about it."

"You got it. Fun girls' day out shopping. I thought we'd start at the outlets in Kittery. They won't be too busy on a weekday."

My stomach gurgled. "Maybe breakfast first? And I want to stop at the apothecary to check in for a second."

Hannah glanced at the clock on the car dashboard. "I'll drop you off, pick up breakfast, then pick you back up again. Sound good? I need to be back to the restaurant before six tonight."

I didn't realize she had time constraints. "Sure. No problem."

I walked through the apothecary and nodded to Mackenzie, who was waiting on Mrs. Williams. Mackenzie shot me a look, and I knew what she was thinking. I continued on and went out back, hoping Alex was still there.

I looked up and the security light was on. The camera was probably recording me as well. Alex's tent was still up, and I wondered if he was still asleep. "Alex," I called softly.

The door to his tent unzipped and he crawled out with a tablet in his hand. "Good morning. The girl inside told me you weren't working today. Thought I'd review the camera footage myself."

"Did anyone wake you last night?" I asked.

"No. Nothing on the video either."

"Interesting." I wondered if it was Elise who tried to break into the shop. "Thank you for watching it."

I turned to leave, but then turned back. "Do you want a job as my security consultant?"

He laughed. "Absolutely not. But I'll keep watch over the apothecary as long as I sleep here."

"Are you sure? We could keep it between us if you wanted—no taxes involved."

He shook his head.

"All right then, if you insist." I pointed to the exterior electrical outlet by the door. "At least use the outlet to charge your tablet."

"I can do that," he said. "I'll keep an eye on everything here, you go enjoy your day off."

I left, thinking there had to be something I could do to compensate him for his help.

I picked up the bag resting on my seat in Hannah's car. "They told me you like éclairs, so I got you one. Not really a breakfast food, but they were certain you wouldn't mind."

"They were right." I took a bite and relaxed into my seat.

"The larger coffee is yours too. I figured you'd need it."

"Thanks. I'm ready to go."

We drove the twenty minutes to the outlet stores, chatting about Hannah's job. I thought she was just the hostess, but when she was working, she was also managing the entire restaurant. Bringing people to their tables was just her way of keeping an eye on everything that was going on.

"I thought we'd start at the watch store," Hannah said.

The store looked expensive, even from the outside. "I'm not sure this store is in my price range," I said.

"Not to worry. I did some reconnaissance work when I was here a few days ago with my mother. They've got some nice, reasonably priced items."

I was here because I trusted her to teach me about Christmas shopping, so I didn't say anything else.

In the store, she led me to a smaller display of tie pins. "You need to get him one of these," she declared.

"Ooookay. Which one?" I asked.

"Honestly, any one would be fine, but you should pick the one you think he'd like the best. It will mean more that way."

I looked at the different tie pins and chains, trying to imagine which one he'd like best. I had no idea.

"Not the chains. You want something with a gemstone," Hannah said.

"I do?"

She nodded. "You're a really nice person, so you probably don't even notice there's a line of women waiting for you two to break up. Christmas presents are an important part of a relationship and, because this is your first one together, your gift absolutely must reflect the depth of your commitment to him and your relationship."

I looked at her, brows furrowed. "That's a lot to put on a present, isn't it?"

"I've seen engagements fall apart due to careless gift choices. You want to give him something with a gemstone so that he considers giving you a gem-based gift the next time he gives you a present."

"I do?"

A sales clerk, who had been eavesdropping, pulled out one display of gold pins. "Your friend is right. Men don't just propose out of thin air. They need to be led to the idea."

I looked at him and saw he was wearing a wedding band. "Is that what happened to you?"

He grinned. "I had no idea what was going on until it was too late."

"This seems manipulative to me. Can't we just pick something nice without it having some sort of meaning? And without him feeling like he's got to get me something nicer?" I took a step back from the counter. "We've only been dating for a few months. It's a little early to be planning our entire future through one gift, isn't it?"

Hannah's smile faded. "Oh. The way the two of you look at each other, I thought you'd already decided he was the man you wanted. If you want to date him without moving the relationship forward any further, then we can get gifts based on that too. I'm sure there's a bookstore around here somewhere."

My heart constricted when Hannah talked about not moving our relationship forward. Had I already decided he was the man for me? I think I had. "It's not that. He said he wanted to take it slow because he had such a messy divorce. I don't want to push him into something he's not ready for."

Hannah put her hand on my arm. "Trust me. I've got a decade of watching people in the restaurant. I've got finely tuned love radar, and this is the right gift for him. We can balance it out with a sweater and something practical too."

I took a leap of faith and decided to trust her. "Okay." I turned back to the tie pins and selected a round garnet with a simple gold bezel. "What do you think about this one?" I asked.

Hannah nodded. "I like it."

I handed the clerk my credit card. "Would you like me to gift wrap it for you?"

"No. I'm meeting my cousins tonight and we're going to wrap all our presents and watch Die Hard."

He rang up my purchase. I glanced at the slip before I put it in my bag. I could afford the gift, but it was a good thing the shop was doing so well.

"Where to next?" I asked.

"We need to get him a sweater and something practical," Hannah said as she held the door open for me.

"Something for his kitchen would be good," I said.

Hannah surveyed the stores near us. "Kitchens R Us"—she pointed—"right over there."

"His kitchen is nice, but his spatulas are old and kind of ugly. I thought I could get him some nicer ones," I said.

Hannah led me to the appropriate aisle, and when I saw the teak utensil set, I knew I'd found the right gift. "These," I said, picking up the box.

"Isabella, those are as much as the tie pin," she said.

I smiled. "I know. And they're practical too. He'll use them every day and hopefully think about me when he does."

She grinned back at me. "Now you're getting the hang of gift giving."

We bought the utensils and drove to our third and last stop, Maine Outdoors. The store was a rambling three-story building that sold everything from delicate china tea cups to guns to jewelry.

"Men's clothing is this way," Hannah said.

I stopped at the display of wool socks. These would make a great gift for Alex. I picked out two pairs. Hannah furrowed her brow at me, but I explained. "They're for someone else."

We chose a black cashmere sweater for Palmer and then our shopping was done. "That wasn't so hard, was it?" Hannah asked me on the drive home.

"I guess not. I've never celebrated Christmas before, so thank you for helping me pick out the right gifts. Yule gifts are much more practical."

I invited her up to my apartment, but she barely had time to get to work.

As I walked up the stairs to my apartment, I could smell something familiar. Aunt Nadia's stuffed mushrooms. My mouth watered, because Hannah and I hadn't stopped for lunch.

I opened the door to see my entire family in my living room, watching a very old Christmas movie. "Hi everyone, what's the movie?"

My mother turned to me. "*Rudolph the Red-Nosed Reindeer*. It was on every year when I was a girl."

That explained the sixties vibe and questionable stop-motion animation. "Next movie, *Die Hard*, a true Christmas classic."

Jules and Jessamin streaked across the back of the couch, part running, part teleporting around the apartment.

Family was wonderful, but would those kittens ever slow down?

The End

We know Prashad and his mother must have had a reunion. Want to see it? Check out this book's bonus scene.
LisaBouchard.com/SIBonus

Books by Lisa Bouchard

Root Cause

Leaf of Faith[1]

What in Carnation[2]

Romaine Calm[3]

No Big Dill

On a Larkspur

Chive Right In

About Thyme

---

1. http://lisabouchard.com/leaf-of-faith-redirection

2. http://lisabouchard.com/what-in-carnation-redirection

3. http://lisabouchard.com/romaine-calm-redirection-page

About the Author

It all started when she learned to read at five. One of her first and favorite memories is of words taped to all the objects in the house. Not long after that, books became the best thing ever and there was no turning back.

She suffered a crisis of confidence in High School and College and decided writing was too difficult, so she earned a degree in Chemistry and later enrolled in a Physics PhD program instead. Three career changes and four children later, she's back to writing and much happier for it.

Now she works from her home office in New Hampshire amid the books, kids, and occasional pets. Visit her at http://LisaBouchard.com.

www.ingramcontent.com/pod-product-compliance
Lightning Source LLC
Chambersburg PA
CBHW071434260626
47170CB00008B/2718